Brides for the Greek Tycoons

Marriages* maid *in Greece!

Business is Cristo's and Niko's first—and only—love. So when marriage becomes necessary to secure the future of their hotel empire, they vow to approach it like any other deal.

Chambermaids Kyra and Sofia are stunned when they receive the biggest tips of their lives—a diamond ring each! Find out what happens when the lives of these Cinderellas go from sweeping the hotel floors to being swept into the tycoons' wealthy jet-set lives in:

The Greek's Ready-Made Wife
Available March 2016

And discover what shocking surprise Sofia has in store for Niko in their story...
Coming soon!

Dear Reader,

Welcome to the first book in the Brides for the Greek Tycoons duet.

Life is never a straight line. The twists and turns can sometimes be painful and other times surprising. The trick is to keep moving forward, because you never know what will be waiting for you around the next corner.

Kyra Pappas has some sad twists to her life and more to come, but she keeps putting one foot in front of the other. She's determined to find new adventures and pieces of her past. When her journey leads her to Greece, to say there are some surprises awaiting her is an understatement, including a very tempting marriage proposal from a Greek tycoon.

Enchanting is the word that comes to mind when Cristo Kiriakas meets Kyra. She has an easy way about her that draws him in and has him thinking that this maid is exactly the person he needs to make his hotel empire legendary. But his plan just might backfire on him when their kiss for the cameras strikes sparks in both of them that are impossible to extinguish.

I hope you'll enjoy Kyra and Cristo's journey as their lives collide at the exclusive Blue Tide Resort in Athens, Greece. Though they both have reasons to want to keep their hearts on the shelf, the Grecian sun and sand combine, creating an intoxicating love potion.

And the story doesn't end here...stay tuned for Niko and Sofia's journey.

Happy reading,

Jennifer Faye

The Greek's Ready-Made Wife

Jennifer Faye

ISBN-13: 978-0-373-74376-6

The Greek's Ready-Made Wife

First North American Publication 2016

This edition published by arrangement with Harlequin Books S.A.

For questions and comments about the quality of this book, please contact us at CustomerService@Harlequin.com.

Printed in U.S.A.

Award-winning author **Jennifer Faye** pens fun, heartwarming romances. Jennifer has won the RT Reviewers' Choice Best Book Award, is a Top Pick author and has been nominated for numerous awards. Now living her dream, she resides with her patient husband, one amazing daughter (the other remarkable daughter is off chasing her own dreams) and two spoiled cats. She'd love to hear from you via her website, jenniferfaye.com.

Books by Jennifer Faye

Harlequin Romance

The Vineyards of Calanetti

Return of the Italian Tycoon

The DeFiore Brothers

The Playboy of Rome
Best Man for the Bridesmaid

Rancher to the Rescue
Snowbound with the Soldier
Safe in the Tycoon's Arms
The Return of the Rebel
A Princess by Christmas
The Prince's Christmas Vow

Visit the Author Profile page
at Harlequin.com for more titles.

For Karen.

Thanks for being such a wonderful, supportive friend and big sis. May your future bring you many amazing adventures both near and far. In case your travels don't take you to Greece, here's an armchair vacation for you.

CHAPTER ONE

"MARRY ME."

Kyra Pappas's breath caught in her throat. She hovered in the doorway of the Governor's suite of the Blue Tide Resort, the housekeeping pass card still clutched in one hand and a pink feather duster in the other. Had she heard correctly? Did someone just utter a marriage proposal?

Talk about bad timing on her part. Still, being a romantic at heart, she couldn't resist trying to catch a quick glimpse of the happy couple before making a hasty exit. Her gaze scanned the room until she stumbled across the most gorgeous man wearing a gray tailored suit, sans the tie.

Wait. She recognized him. Yesterday, he'd returned to this suite just as she'd finished freshening everything. They'd chatted briefly about her being American. He'd inquired whether she enjoyed working at the resort. As their conversation had progressed, he'd mentioned some local sites she should visit while in Greece. He'd certainly seemed nice enough.

But right now, he was staring directly at her. Why

would he be looking at her when he was in the middle of a marriage proposal? Kyra glanced around. They were alone. And the television was turned off. How could that be?

And then a thought struck her. Surely he wasn't posing the question to her. The breath caught in her throat. No. Impossible.

Her puzzled gaze studied the man with the tanned face. She could stare at him for hours. His dark wavy hair made her long to run her fingers through it, while his startling azure-blue eyes seemed to see all. He kept staring at her as though he expected her to respond. Perhaps she hadn't heard him correctly.

"I'm sorry. What did you say?"

His dark brows drew together as his forehead wrinkled. "I…asked if you'd marry me."

He really had proposed. This stranger wanted to marry her? To say she was caught off guard was akin to saying the Hope diamond was just another trinket.

For just the briefest moment, she imagined what it'd be like if he was serious. Until now, no one had spoken those words to her. On those occasional Saturday nights when she was home alone, she wondered if she'd ever fall in love. But she wasn't desperate enough to fall for the charming words of a stranger—however sexy he may be.

Besides, the last thing she wanted was to be tied down—not now when she'd just embarked on an adventure to find her extended family. She had other priorities and love wasn't one of them. It wasn't even on her lengthy to-do list.

She studied the serious expression on the man's face. He certainly didn't seem to be making light of his proposal. So then why had he proposed marriage to a total stranger? Was he delusional? Or had he made some sort of ridiculous wager with his buddies?

"Are you feeling all right, sir?" Her gaze panned the room again, this time a bit more slowly, looking for an open liquor bottle or a hidden camera. Anything to explain his odd behavior.

"I…I'm not exactly handling this well." He rubbed a hand over his clean-shaven jaw. "I must admit that I've never proposed to anyone before."

"Is this some sort of bet? A joke?"

His face turned gravely serious. "Certainly not. This is a serious business proposition. One that could benefit you handsomely."

Which was it? A marriage proposal? Or a business proposition? Kyra's mouth opened but nothing came out. Perhaps it was for the best. The man must have started drinking early that day even though she couldn't find any signs of it. The best thing she could do was beat a hasty retreat. She took a step back.

"Don't look so scared. I'm really not that bad." He sent her a lazy smile that made her stomach quiver. "I'm usually so much better at these things. Give me a moment to explain."

"I have work to do." She'd heard about rich people having weird tendencies. She kept a firm eye on him as she took another step back. "I…I'll stop back later and…um, freshen up your room."

"Please, don't go." He took a few quick steps toward her.

She held up a hand to stop him. "Don't come any closer or I'll scream."

"Relax. I won't hurt you. I promise." He rubbed the back of his neck. "I'm sorry. I'm really making a mess of things. I guess I should be relieved this isn't a real proposal."

She eyed him up to see if at last he was being on the level. The guilty puppy look on his face was so cute and tugged at her sympathies. He must be in a real bind to suggest something so preposterous. "Apology accepted. Now I really should get back to work."

"Aren't you at least curious about my proposal?"

Of course she was. Who wouldn't be? She studied the man a little more, noticing how the top couple of buttons on his slate blue button-down shirt were undone. It gave her the slightest hint of his muscular chest. She swallowed hard. To keep from staring, she diverted her gaze. On his arm, she spotted a fancy wristwatch. She wouldn't be surprised to find it was a Rolex.

He looked every inch a successful businessman right down to his freshly polished shoes. A man who was used to getting what he wanted. A man who made calculated decisions. And somehow he'd decided she would do for his plan. Interesting.

"Yes, I'm curious." She crossed her arms to keep from fidgeting. What would it hurt to hear him out? "Go ahead. I'm listening."

"Wouldn't you rather come inside and have a seat where you'll be more comfortable?"

"I'm good here." Until she had a clue what was going on, she was staying close to the open door. After all, she grew up in New York City. Her mother taught her at an early age not to trust strangers. Although, she didn't know if her mother would extend that warning to dashing billionaires or not, but Kyra didn't find wealth and class as important as her mother did.

He shifted his weight from one foot to the other. "I realize we don't know each other very well. But I enjoyed our conversation yesterday. You seem like a very interesting young woman, and you have a way of putting people at ease."

She did? She'd never been told that before. "Thank you. But I don't understand why you're, uh, proposing to me."

"I'm trying to secure a very important business deal. The problem is the seller is an older gentleman and a traditionalist. He has certain expectations that I currently fail to meet. Such as being a family man."

He wants to play house with me?

No way. She wasn't doing this. She didn't even know his name. "I'm not the right person."

"You're exactly who I need." His eyes gleamed with excitement.

She made an obvious point of glancing at the time on her phone. "I really need to get going. I have a lot of rooms to clean today."

"You don't have to worry. I'll vouch for you."

What an odd thing to say, but then again, this whole episode could easily be classified as bizarre. Just so she knew who to avoid in the future, she asked, "Who are you?"

His dark brows rose. "You don't know?"

She shook her head. The only thing she knew about him was that no one had a right to look that sexy. "Would I have asked if I knew?"

"True. Allow me to introduce myself. My name is Cristo Kiriakas."

His name did ring a bell—a very loud bell. It took a moment until she was able to place it. Kyra gasped. He was her boss—the owner of the Glamour Hotel and Casino chain that included the newly built Blue Tide Resort. She would have known it was him if only she'd done her homework. This was, after all, the Governor's suite—the best in the resort.

"Nice to meet you, Mr. Kiriakas. I…I'm Kyra Pappas. I didn't recognize you."

"Don't look so worried." He spoke in a calm, soothing tone. "I didn't expect you to recognize me. And please, call me Cristo. My father insists on going by Mr. Kiriakas. So every time you say that name, I'll be looking over my shoulder for my father."

"Sorry, sir. Um. Cristo. You can call me Kyra." At this particularly awkward juncture, she supposed the wisest thing to do regarding her employment while in a foreign country was to reason with the man. "Does my job hinge on me playing along with your wedding plans?"

"No, it doesn't. You don't have to worry. Your job is safe."

She wasn't sure about that. "Surely you have a girlfriend—someone close to you—to marry."

His jaw tensed and a muscle in his cheek twitched. "Yes, I could find someone to marry for real, but the truth is I don't want to be married. Not for keeps."

"Then why jump through all of these hoops? You seem rich enough to do as you please."

"I wish it were as easy as that. But having money doesn't mean things come to you any easier. Some things are still unobtainable without help."

Kyra had lived with money and without money. She found that both lifestyles had their positives and negatives. But she didn't know that other people had similar opinions. Her mother seemed to think that having money was the only important thing in life. And if you no longer had money, like her and her mother, then you pretended as if you did. Kyra didn't subscribe to that way of thinking, but after going round and round with her mother, she knew trying to change her mother's mind was a waste of time.

Kyra eyed up Cristo. "And you want my help to create a paper marriage so you can conclude a business deal?" She struggled to get this all straight in her mind. "And when the deal's complete, we'll go our separate ways?"

"Yes." He smiled as though relieved that she finally grasped what he was saying. "But it's not just any business deal. It'll be the biggest of my career. It'll change everything."

The conviction in his voice surprised her. Even though she didn't quite understand the importance of this deal, she felt bad for him. Why would anyone have to propose to a stranger in order to do business? No one should marry someone they didn't love heart, body and soul. For any reason.

Perhaps he needed a bit of coaxing in order to see things clearly. "There has to be another way."

He shook his head. "If there was, trust me, I would have done it by now."

She paused for a moment and gave his predicament a bit of thought. "Well, if marriage is so important, why can't you just have a fake fiancée? Wouldn't that save you a lot of trouble?"

Not that she was applying for the position—even though his blue eyes were mesmerizing and his mouth looked as though it could do the most delicious things. The fact was she'd come to Greece with her own agenda. And getting caught up in someone else's drama would only delay making life better for her and her mother.

* * *

This lady was sharp.

That was a definite bonus.

Cristo smiled. He knew from the moment he'd met Kyra that there was something special about her. And it went much deeper than her silky dark hair with long bangs that framed her big brown eyes. The rest of her hair was pulled back in a ponytail. He imagined how seductive she'd look with her hair loose and flowing over her shoulders.

However, his interest in her went beyond her good looks. From the moment they'd met, he'd noticed the warmth in her smile and the ease in her manner. Who knew she'd end up being the answer to his problems? He hadn't—not until this morning when he submitted his final proposal to the Stravos Trust to purchase its hotel chain. It had been summarily rejected without review.

He knew then and there that he was going to have to play by the off-the-wall rules laid out by the reclusive billionaire Nikolaos Stravos, whether he liked it or not. And he most certainly did not like having his business deals hinge on his personal life.

Although, Kyra's suggestion of an engagement might make the arrangement a bit more tolerable. An engagement wouldn't necessitate the use of attorneys and an ironclad prenuptial agreement. It'd be all very neat and tidy.

His gaze met and held hers. He needed more information in order to make this work. "How long have you been working at the Blue Tide? I don't remember seeing you around here before yesterday."

"That's because yesterday was my first day. I used to work in the New York hotel."

"Did you work there long?"

"A few years."

"And it was in housekeeping?"

She nodded, but the way she worried her bottom lip was a dead giveaway that she was leaving something out. If he was going to trust her with this important deal, he had to know what she was leaving out. "What aren't you saying?"

Her gaze met his as though deciding if she should trust him or not. After a few seconds, she said, "I'm currently taking online courses in international hotel management."

"I don't understand. Why would you be hesitant to tell me that?"

She laced her fingers together. "I didn't want you to think I was ungrateful for my current position."

He smiled at her, hoping to ease her obvious discomfort. "The thought never would have crossed my mind. I encourage all of my employees to further themselves. In fact, we have in-house training sessions periodically."

"I know. I checked into them."

Again, she was leaving something out, but he was pretty sure of what she was hesitant to say. "But we don't offer the classes you are interested in. And if you don't mind me asking, what might that be?"

She straightened her thin shoulders and tilted up her chin. "Property manager."

Of course. He should have known. There was a get-it-done spirit to her. "I have no doubt that you will succeed."

Her lips lifted into a warm smile. "Thank you."

So she had drive. He respected that. But there was still so much that he didn't know about her. The cautious side of him said to pull her personnel file, but there wasn't time. However, his manager made a practice of thoroughly investigating prospective employees. She must have a clean history or she wouldn't be here.

"I enjoyed our conversation yesterday. You're a very insightful young woman. And I would consider it a huge favor if you were to help me out with my business issue."

The panic vacated her eyes as her rigid stance eased. "I really do like my job with housekeeping. It allows me time to, uh…sightsee and stuff."

"Will you at least consider my proposition?"

"I have. And the answer is no. I'm sorry, but you'll have to find yourself someone else to play the part." She started out the door.

"Please think it over." He threw out an outrageous dollar figure that put a pause in her step. "I really need your assistance."

He was running out of time.

And options.

CHAPTER TWO

THE MOST LOGICAL thing to do right now was to keep walking.

Yet there was that note of desperation in Cristo's voice. Something told her that he didn't say please very often.

Kyra hesitated, her back still to him. Why was this most bizarre plan so important to him? What secrets was he holding back? And why did she care? This wasn't her problem.

"If I didn't really need your help, I wouldn't have proposed this arrangement. I swear." Weariness laced his every syllable. "I will make it worth your while. If that wasn't enough money, name your price."

Why did it always come back to money? "I'm not for sale."

She headed straight for her cart of cleaning supplies. She dropped the feather duster back in its proper spot. Her curiosity got the best of her. She glanced over her shoulder to see if Cristo had followed her into the hallway.

He hadn't. She breathed easier. What in the world did they put in the water around here? Because there was no way that whole scene was normal. After all, they were strangers. No one would ever believe they were a couple.

As she prepared to push her cart to the next suite, she recalled the large dollar figure he'd named and the offer to make it bigger if necessary. Okay, she may not be a gold digger, but that didn't mean she'd turn her nose up at some extra income. But could she really play the part of his fiancée?

Could she pretend to be something she wasn't?

Wouldn't that make her a hypocrite?

Kyra paused in front of the next suite. She recalled how many times she'd gone round and round with her mother in the past year since her father's death about putting on a show for her mother's country-club friends. When her father had died, so had their silver-spoon lifestyle.

Kyra felt sorry for her mother—first losing the love of her life and then having to go back to work after twenty-plus years as a stay-at-home mom. With her mother buried beneath a mountain of debt, Kyra had moved back in to help meet the mortgage payments. And though this new position in Greece took her away from home, Kyra reconciled it with the fact that it paid more so she could send more money home.

The one other reason Kyra had taken the position was to help her mother—even if her mother swore she didn't need help. With her father gone, her mother was depressed and lonely as her country-club friends had less and less to do with her. With no other family in New York, Kyra had hoped to locate her father's extended family. If she could forge bonds with them, maybe she could make a life for her and her mother here in Greece. By once again being part of a warm, supportive family, perhaps her mother wouldn't feel so alone.

One thought after the next rolled around in Kyra's mind as she cleaned the remaining suites on the floor. All the while, her thoughts moved back and forth between doing what she felt was right and earning enough money to help her mother, who had always been there for her. Did Kyra's principles outweigh her duty to help her mother?

And the fact she was in Greece gave her the freedom to make decisions she wouldn't normally make. Being thousands of miles from New York City meant her chance of running into anyone she knew was slim to none. Well, there was one person at the Blue Tide that knew her, her best friend, Sofia Moore. But Sofia would keep her secret.

Speaking of her best friend, Kyra could really use some advice right now. If anyone could make sense of this very odd opportunity, it would be Sofia. Once the last suite on the floor had been put to rights, Kyra paused next to the large window overlooking the private cove. She pulled out her phone. Her fingers moved rapidly over the screen.

Mop&Glow007 (Kyra): Hey, you're never going to believe this. I met someone.

She just couldn't bring herself to admit that she'd been proposed to by a stranger, only to learn later it was their boss. Somehow, it sounded desperate on his part. And she felt sorry for Cristo.

Seconds turned into a minute, then two, and still no response. Where was Sofia? Probably still cleaning the exclusive bungalows that lined the beach. But Sofia always had her phone close at hand.

MaidintheShade347 (Sofia): As in a guy?

Mop&Glow007 (Kyra): Yes.

MaidintheShade347 (Sofia): What? But how? You swore off guys.

Mop&Glow007 (Kyra): I know. But he found me.

MaidintheShade347 (Sofia): And it was love at first sight?

Mop&Glow007 (Kyra): Not quite. More like a business deal.

MaidintheShade347 (Sofia): He offered to pay you to be his girlfriend?

Mop&Glow007 (Kyra): Yep. A bundle.

MaidintheShade347 (Sofia): You can't be serious. Is this a joke?

Mop&Glow007 (Kyra): No joke.

MaidintheShade347 (Sofia): Is he cute?

Mop&Glow007 (Kyra): Very.

MaidintheShade347 (Sofia): Is he rich?

Mop&Glow007 (Kyra): Very.

MaidintheShade347 (Sofia): And you accepted?

Mop&Glow007 (Kyra): Not yet.

MaidintheShade347 (Sofia): Why not?

Mop&Glow007 (Kyra): You think I should really consider this idea?

MaidintheShade347 (Sofia): Sure. It's not like you have anything better waiting in the wings.

Mop&Glow007 (Kyra): Thx for making me sound so pathetic.

MaidintheShade347 (Sofia): Oops! My bad. Go for it. Gotta run. Talk soon.

Kyra blinked and read Sofia's last message again. *Go for it.* Was she serious? Then again, ever since Sofia had caught her boyfriend in bed with another woman, Sofia's attitude had changed drastically. When it came to men, she didn't trust them and she refused to get serious, but she was open to having a good time. Kyra was happy that Sofia had regained her spirit and was getting out there and trying different things. But should Kyra do the same? Then again, wasn't that part of the reason for this trip to Greece? Trying something different?

Maybe it was time she quit living life so conservatively. Maybe it wouldn't hurt to color outside the lines, just a little. Mr. Kiriakas's tanned, chiseled face formed in her mind. It certainly wouldn't be so bad being his fiancée for a night or two. She had enjoyed talking to him the other day, and when he smiled, it made her stomach quiver. Sofia was right. She had nothing to lose. It might actually be fun.

Before she could chicken out, she turned in her supplies and rushed to the small apartment she shared with Sofia in the employee housing. Once she had showered and changed into yellow capris and a pink cotton top, she rushed to his suite. She didn't have any idea if he'd still be there.

Her knuckles rapped on the door. She hadn't been this nervous since she came home from school with a below average grade on her report card. She didn't know why she was so jittery. Cristo certainly was nice enough. Besides, this whole thing was his idea.

The door swung open and there before her stood her almost-fiancé, all six foot plus of toned muscle. She tilted her chin upward in order to meet his gaze. "I...I thought over what you said earlier, and I have a few questions for you."

He hesitated and then swung the door open. "Come in."

She glanced around, making sure they were alone. As she did so, she took in the difference in decor between this suite and the other units. For one thing, the standard black upholstered furniture was leather in this suite. The art on the walls consisted of prints in the other suites, but in here everything was original, one-of-a-kind paintings. And lastly, the suite definitely had a lived-in feel—a sense of hominess to it.

Behind her, she could hear the door snick shut. It was just the two of them, alone. Suddenly Kyra didn't feel quite so confident, so ready to strike a business deal. Right now, even the memory of Sofia's encouraging words sounded foolish. After all, she didn't go out on limbs and take big risks. She liked to play it safe.

Cristo cleared his throat. "Should I take your presence to mean you've changed your mind about my offer?"

She forced her gaze to meet his. "It depends on your answers to my questions."

"What would you like to know?"

Comfortable that she'd left herself an out, should she need it, she leveled her shoulders. "The pretense of being your fiancée, it would only be a show for others, right? You don't want me to, um…sleep with you?"

"No. No. Nothing like that."

She breathed a little easier. "And how long would I have to pretend to be your fiancée?"

"I'll be honest with you. I'm not sure."

"So this is going to take longer than a day or two?"

He hesitated. "Yes, it will. But only until my business deal is concluded. It could be a few weeks or as long as a couple of months—"

"Months?" Kyra shook her head. *No way.* He was simply asking too much of her. "That's not possible. I can't pretend to be your fiancée for that long."

"Are you planning to return to the States before then?"

The easiest way out of this mess was to say yes, but in truth she wasn't leaving Greece until she had a chance to track down her father's family. And since she didn't have a starting point, she didn't know how long that would take her. "No. I'm not leaving yet. I…I have things to do here."

"Anything I can help you with?" When she cast him a skeptical look, he rushed to add, "There are no strings attached to that offer. I like you. You make me smile, and it's been a while since anyone did that. Whether you agree to this plan or not, I'd like to help you out, if I can."

Now, why did he have to go and do that? It would have been so much easier to say no to a man who was pushy and arrogant. None of those descriptions quite fit Cristo Kiriakas. He was more like a really hot, Grecian…gentleman.

"Thank you. That's very kind of you. But not necessary."

"It may not be necessary, but I'd like to help. What has you here in Greece?"

His eyes told her that he was serious. He was really interested in her. So what would it hurt to open up and share a little with him?

"I'm here to find my extended family, or what's left of it." Cristo's brows rose with surprise, encouraging her to continue. "My father passed away a little more than a year ago. He'd always wondered about his extended family and had promised one day we'd take a trip here to see what we could learn. Now that he can't finish our research, I'm taking up where he left off."

"It sounds important."

"It is. For me, that is. My mother doesn't understand my need to do this." In fact, her mother had done everything in her power to curtail Kyra's trip, from pleading to offering up excuse after excuse until she finally resorted to a big guilt trip.

"I know some people who go by the name Pappas—"

"You do?" Could it really be this simple? "How do I find them?"

He held up a hand. "Slow down. Pappas isn't exactly a unique name."

"Oh." She'd known that from her research, but after hitting so many dead ends, she just wanted some hope.

"Do you have much family in the States?" Cristo's voice halted her thoughts.

"There's just me and my mother. The rest of my mother's family, small as it was, passed away. I thought my mother would understand my need to find out more about my past, especially after losing my father. But all she did was get angry and resentful any time I brought up a trip to Greece. Finally, I just stopped trying to make her understand."

"So you thought by taking a job here that you would have the perfect excuse to investigate your family's roots?"

She nodded. At the same time, her phone chimed. Expecting it to be Sofia, she grabbed it from her pocket. The caller ID said Mom. Kyra forwarded the call to her voice mail before slipping the phone back in her pocket.

"If you need to answer that, go ahead."

"It's not important. I'll get it later." The last thing Kyra needed right now was to talk to her mother in front of Cristo—a man who had a way of short-circuiting her thoughts with just a look. No man had ever had that kind of power over her. And she wasn't sure she liked it, but another part of her found him exciting—exhilarating—unlike any man she'd ever known.

"Suit yourself." He moved to the fully stocked refrigerator and removed a bottle of water. He glanced over his shoulder at her. "Would you care for one, too?"

What would it hurt? After all, he was being nice enough and she was a bit thirsty. "Yes. Thank you."

Her phone chimed again. It wasn't like her mother to call right back. Kyra did a quick time change in her head and realized that her mother should be at her second part-time job. Perhaps she was just checking in on one of her breaks.

When Cristo handed over the bottle, their fingers brushed. Their gazes met and held. The breath caught in her throat. She'd never gazed into eyes so intense, so full of energy. She'd heard people talk about instant attraction but she hadn't really known what they were talking about until now. Sure, she'd noticed some really good-looking guys, but they'd always been easily forgotten. Something told her that Cristo would not be so easily dismissed.

He stepped back. "If you'd like something to eat, I could order from the restaurant downstairs."

"No, thanks. I'm fine." With the flutter of nerves in her stomach, there was no way she could eat a bite of anything. “About the arrangement. Will we have to be seen in public together?”

“Definitely.” His gaze narrowed. “Will that be a problem? Do you have a boyfriend?”

“No. No boyfriend.” She glanced down at her casual clothes and then at his designer suit. “But I don’t have anything appropriate in my wardrobe.”

“No worries. A new wardrobe and accessories will be part of your benefits package.”

Just like that he could arrange for a new, designer wardrobe without even a thought. Wow. How much was this man worth?

With a slight tremor in her hand, she pressed the cold bottle to her lips and took a small sip. She tried to recall the other questions she’d wanted to ask, but her mind drew a blank. At least she’d asked the important ones.

He walked over and placed his bottle on the bar. “I know this is rushing things, but I really need to know your answer to my offer.”

“You definitely don’t give a girl much time to weigh her options.”

His voice grew deeper. “Maybe I just don’t want to give you time to find an excuse to back out on me. I can already tell you’re going to make my life interesting. You, my dear, are quite intriguing. And I find that refreshing.”

“Is that all you find attractive?” The flirtatious words slipped over her lips before they registered in her mind.

His eyes lit up as the heat of embarrassment swirled in her chest and rose up her neck. What was she doing? She barely even knew this man. And yet, she was drawn to him like a moth to a flame, but if she wasn't cautious, she'd get burned.

"It's definitely not the only attractive aspect of this arrangement. Not even close—"

"The money you offered, is it still part of the deal?"

He nodded.

"And can you pay me weekly?" She wanted to pay down the mortgage as soon as possible.

His brows rose. "If that's what you'd like."

"It is."

She made the mistake of gazing into his eyes and noting that he looked at her with genuine interest. Did she really intrigue him? Her heart fluttered. Would it be so bad to have a gorgeous fiancé for just a bit? After all, you only live once. What did it hurt to have a little adventure?

And aside from the money, he'd mentioned helping her to search for her family roots. Now she had to make certain it was part of the deal. "And you agree to assist me in the search for my extended family?"

"I do."

She stepped up to him and extended her hand. "You have yourself a fiancée."

Instead of accepting her hand and shaking it, he lifted it to his lips. His feathery light kiss sent waves of delicious sensations coursing through her body. Much too soon he released her.

"When, um…do we start?" She hoped her voice sounded calmer than she felt at the moment.

"Right now. You have a wedding to plan and we need to get to know each other much better if we are going to convince others that we're a genuine couple."

Her phone chimed. It was her mother again. Something was definitely wrong. Kyra couldn't deny it any longer. "Excuse me for a moment while I answer this."

He nodded in understanding.

Kyra moved toward the wall of windows that overlooked the white sandy beach and aquamarine water. She pressed the phone to her ear. Before she could utter a word, she heard her mother's voice.

"Kyra, why didn't you answer your phone? I didn't call to talk to your voice mail. Do you even listen to your messages? If you had, you'd know this is important—"

"Mom, stop. Take a breath and then tell me what's the matter."

"Everything."

Her mother had a way of blowing things out of proportion. *Please let this be one of those times.* "Mom, are you all right? You aren't in the hospital, are you?"

"The hospital? Why would I be there?"

Kyra exhaled a relieved sigh. "Just tell me what's wrong."

"My life. It's over. You have to come home."

Not melodramatic at all. "I'm sure it's not that bad."

"How would you know? You don't even know what's the matter."

Kyra fully expected this would be another engineered guilt trip. "Mom, just tell me."

"I would if you'd quit interrupting."

Keeping her back to Cristo, Kyra rolled her eyes. Why did talking to her mother always have to be an exercise in patience? Her father must have had more patience than a saint. "I'm listening now."

"They let me go. Can you believe that? After all I did for them. Is there no longer any such thing as loyalty and respect?"

"Who let you go?"

"The cleaning company. They said they lost some contracts and had to downsize. How can they do that? Don't they know I have bills to pay?" Her mother's voice cracked with emotion. "Kyra, you have to come home right away. I need you."

She should have known it'd come round to this. "I can't. I have a job to do."

"But we're going to lose our home." There was an awkward pause. "I don't know what I'm going to do. I'm all alone."

"Don't worry." Kyra may not agree with everything her mother said and did, but she still loved her.

And her mother didn't deserve to lose her home—no one did. "You won't lose your home. I'll help you."

Kyra, realizing that she'd said too much in front of Cristo, wound up the phone conversation. She promised to call her mother back soon.

Not sure how much Cristo had overheard, her body tensed. Her mother always did have the most amazing timing. Still, there was no undoing what had been done.

She turned to him. He was staring at her with questions reflected in his eyes. She couldn't blame him. If the roles had been reversed, she would have been curious, as well. "Sorry. That was my mother."

"I take it there's a problem."

Kyra really didn't want to get into this with him. "There is, but it's nothing I can't deal with."

He arched a dark brow. "Are you sure about that? I mean, if you have to leave Greece, it's best that we end our arrangement now—"

"No. That won't be necessary." And she didn't add that the money he'd been willing to pay her for her time would be a huge help with her mother's plight. Her doubts about whether she really wanted to move forward with this plan had just been overturned. She owed this to her mother. "I'm all yours—so to speak."

CHAPTER THREE

KYRA WAS ALL HIS.

Cristo couldn't deny that he liked the sound of those words. In fact, that wasn't the only thing he could imagine passing by that tempting mouth.

Cristo gave himself a mental shake. What was he doing daydreaming about this woman? He knew better than to think of romance. He'd witnessed firsthand what happened when the romance turned cold. His parents were like the king and queen of Frostville. He got frostbite every time they were in the same room. He refused to end up unhappy like them.

Cristo cleared his throat. "Maybe we should start this relationship over." He held out his hand to her. "Hi. I'm Cristo."

She slipped her slender hand in his. He immediately noticed the coolness of her skin. She was undeniably nervous. That was good because he was, too.

Her fingers tightened around his hand. "Hi. My name's Kyra. I have the feeling this is going to be quite an adventure."

He had the same feeling but for other reasons, none that he wanted to delve into at the moment. "Let me know whatever you'll need to make this arrangement as pleasant as possible."

As she pulled her hand away, surprise reflected in her eyes. "You make it sound like I've just released the genie from the magic lantern."

"Not exactly. But I do want you to be comfortable during our time together." Cristo knew how thorough Stravos was with his background checks of potential business associates. "I need this engagement to be as authentic as possible. Don't spare any detail or expense."

"What expense?"

"For our wedding."

"You're serious? You really want me to plan a wedding that's never going to happen?"

He nodded. "You have no idea what type of man I'm dealing with. Nikolaos Stravos is sharp and thorough."

"But if people know about this engagement, how are you going to explain it when we break up?"

"I thought about it and we'll handle it just like everyone else who calls off their wedding. We'll tell people it's an amicable split and we'd appreciate everyone respecting our privacy during this difficult time."

"That may be fine for the public but not for close friends and relatives."

"I've thought of that, too." He smiled, liking having all of the answers. "We'll tell them we couldn't agree on kids. You want a couple and I want none."

"Are you serious?"

He nodded. "It's a legitimate reason with no associated scandal. We won't be the first couple to break up over the subject."

She paused as though giving the subject serious consideration. "I suppose it'll work."

He cleared his throat. "It's the truth, at least partially. I'm too busy for a family." That wasn't the only reason he'd written off being a father, but it was all he was willing to share at the moment. "If we're going to do this, we have to make the relationship authentic to hold up under scrutiny. Starting with you moving in here."

"But…but I can't. I told you I'm not sleeping with you."

"And I don't expect you to. But if people are supposed to believe we're getting married, then they'll expect us to be intimate." When she opened her mouth to protest, he held up his hand silencing her. "We only have to give people the impression. Nothing more. Is that going to be a problem?"

Her worried gaze met his. He couldn't blame her for hesitating. He knew he was asking a lot of her. But he was stuck between the proverbial rock and a hard place. She'd been a really good sport, until now.

He had to give her an out. He owed her that much.

"It's okay if you want to back out. I will totally understand."

For a moment, he thought she had indeed changed her mind—that she was going to head for the door and never look back. His body tensed. He didn't have a plan B. He'd only devised this plan, such as it was, on the spur of the moment.

When she spoke, her voice was surprisingly calm and held a note of certainty. "You're right. People will grow suspicious if we don't act like a normal engaged couple. But won't people talk about me being a maid?"

He shook his head. "You've only been on the job for two days, and I'm guessing you haven't met many guests."

"No. Not really."

"Good. I wouldn't worry." She glanced around the suite as though trying to decide how they would coexist. He could ease her mind. "Don't worry. There's a guest room with a lock on the door. But I'm sure you probably already know that."

She nodded. "When do you want me to move in?"

"Now. I'll send someone to gather your stuff. It'll be less obvious if you aren't lugging around your suitcases. Are you staying in the employee accommodations?"

She gave him the unit number. "But I…I need to tell my friend."

"Remember, this arrangement has to be kept strictly between us. You can't tell anyone about it or it'll never work. Nikolaos Stravos has contacts everywhere."

"Understood."

"Good. You stay here and I'll have your luggage delivered to you." Her mouth opened, then closed. "Is there a problem?"

She shook her head. "I'll have Sofia toss my things together."

"Good. Because we have big plans tonight."

Was this really happening?

Dressed in a maroon designer dress from the overpriced boutique in the lobby, Kyra held on to Cristo's arm. She was glad to have something to steady her as her knees felt like gelatin. Her hair had been professionally styled and her makeup had been applied by a cosmetologist. It was certainly a lot of fuss for a dinner date. What was Cristo up to?

She highly doubted she'd be able to eat a bite. Her stomach was a ball of nerves. They paused at the entrance of the resort's High Tide Restaurant. The place was dimly lit with candles on each table. Gentle, soothing music played in the background, but it wasn't having any effect on Kyra.

Numerous heads turned as the maître d' escorted them to a corner table. Cristo made a point of greeting people. It was like being on the arm of royalty as everyone seemed to know him. At last at their table, Cristo pulled out her chair. Quite the gentleman. She was impressed.

He took the seat across from her. “Relax. You look beautiful.”

Heat warmed her cheeks. She knew she shouldn’t let his words get to her. Everything he said and did tonight was all an act. “You look quite handsome yourself.”

“Thank you.” He sat up a little straighter as a smile reflected in his eyes. “Can I order you some wine? Maybe it’ll help you relax.”

“Is it that obvious?” She worried her bottom lip while fidgeting with the silverware.

He reached out to her. His hand engulfed hers, stilling it. “Just a little.”

Her gaze met his before glancing down at their clasped hands. She attempted to pull away, but he tightened his grip and stroked the back of her hand with his thumb, sending wave after wave of delicious sensations coursing through her body.

She struggled to come up with a coherent thought. “What are you doing?”

“Trying to get my fiancée to relax and enjoy herself. We don’t want anyone wondering why you look so unhappy, do we?”

“Oh.” She glanced around, making sure they weren’t being watched. Thankfully, no one seemed to notice the bumpy start to their evening. Cristo was right, she needed to do better at holding up her end of this deal—no matter how unnerving it was being in this dimly lit restaurant at a candlelit table with the most handsome man in the room while trying to remain detached.

After making sure the server wasn't within earshot, she said softly, "Would you mind releasing my hand?"

Cristo's brows lifted, but he didn't say a word as he pulled away. She immediately noticed the coldness where he'd once been touching her. She shoved the unsettling thought aside as she picked up the menu. *Just act normal.*

"Would you like me to recommend something?"

Her gaze lifted over the edge of the menu, which was written in both Greek and English. "Do you have it memorized?"

"Would it be bad if I said I did?"

"Really?" He nodded and she added, "You take a hands-on boss to a whole new level."

His eyes twinkled as his smile grew broader and she suddenly realized that her words could be taken out of context. It'd been a total slip of the tongue. Hadn't it?

"The chef's specialty is seafood."

She forced her gaze to remain on the menu instead of continuing to stare into Cristo's eyes. Though her gaze focused on the scrolled entrées, none of it registered in her mind. "I'm not really a seafood fan."

"Beef? Salad? Pasta—"

"Pasta sounds good." Especially on a nervous stomach.

Cristo talked her through the menu. His voice was soothing and little by little she began to relax. She decided on chicken Alfredo and Cristo surprised her by ordering the same thing.

"You didn't have to do that."

His brows drew together. "Do what?"

"Order the same thing just to make me feel better."

A smile warmed his face. "Perhaps we just have similar tastes."

Perhaps they did. Now, why did that warm a spot in her chest? It wasn't as if this was a real date. Everything was a case of make-believe. Did that include his words?

He didn't give her time to contemplate the question as he continued the conversation, moving on to subjects such as how the weather compared to New York, and the differences between the Blue Tide Resort and his flagship business, the Glamour Hotel in New York City, where she'd previously worked.

She appreciated that he was trying so hard to put her at ease. It was as though they were on a genuine date. He even flirted with her, making her laugh. Kyra was thoroughly impressed. She didn't think he would be this patient or kind. She had to keep reminding herself that it was all a show. But the more he talked, the harder it was to remember this wasn't a date.

Much later, the meal was over and Cristo stared at her in the wavering candlelight. "How about dessert?"

She shook her head as she pressed a hand to her full stomach. "Not me. I'm going to have to run extra long tomorrow just to wear off a fraction of these calories."

He pressed his elbows to the table and leaned forward. "You don't have to worry. You look amazing. Enjoy tonight. Consider it a new beginning for both of us."

A new beginning? Why did it seem as though he was trying to seduce her tonight? Maybe because he was. She was going to have to be extra careful around this charmer.

"The dinner was great. Thank you so much. But I honestly can't eat another bite."

A frown pulled at his lips. "I have something special ordered just for you."

"You do?" No one had ever gone to this much trouble for her, pretend or real.

He nodded. "Will you at least sample it? I wouldn't want the chef to be insulted."

"Of course." Then she had an idea. "Why don't you share it with me?"

"You have a deal." He signaled to the waiter that they were ready for the final course. It seemed almost instantaneous when the waiter appeared. He approached with a solitary cupcake.

It wasn't until the waiter had placed the cupcake in front of her that she realized there was a diamond ring sitting atop the large dollop of frosting. The jewel was big. No, it was huge.

Kyra gasped.

The waiter immediately backed away. Cristo moved from his chair and retrieved the ring. What was he up to? Was it a mistake that he was going to correct? Because no one purchased a ring that big for someone who was just their fake fiancée. At least no rational person.

Cristo dropped to his knee next to her chair. Her mouth opened but no words came out. Was he going to propose to her? Right here? In front of everyone?

A noticeable silence fell over the room as one by one people turned and stared at them. The only sound now was the quickening beat of her heart.

Cristo gazed into her eyes. "Kyra, you stumbled into my life, reminding me of all that I'd been missing. You showed me that there's more to life than business. You make me smile. You make me laugh. I can only hope to make you nearly as happy. Will you make me the happiest man in the world and marry me?"

The words were perfect. The sentiment was everything a woman could hope for. She knew this was where she was supposed to say *yes*, but even though her jaw moved, the words were trapped in her throat. Instead, she nodded and blinked back the involuntary rush of emotions. Someday she hoped the right guy would say those words to her and mean them.

Cristo took her hand in his. She was shaking and there wasn't a darn thing she could do at that moment to stop it. Perhaps she should have realized he had this planned all along, what with her fancy dress and the stylist. If he wanted a surprised reaction, he got it.

Who'd have thought Cristo had a romantic streak? He'd created the most amazing evening. Something told her she would never forget this night. She couldn't wait to tell Sofia. She was going to be so upset that she missed it.

Cristo stood and then helped Kyra to her feet. As though under a spell, she leaned into him. There was an intensity in his gaze that had her staring back, unable to turn away. Her pulse raced and her heart tumbled in her chest.

When his gaze dipped to her mouth, the breath caught in her throat. He was going to kiss her. His hands lifted and cupped her face. Their lips were just inches apart.

She should pull back. Turn away. Instead, she stood there anxiously waiting for his touch. Would it be gentle and teasing? Or would it be swift and demanding?

"You complete me." Those softly spoken words shattered her last bit of reality. She gave in to the fantasy. He was her Prince Charming and for tonight she was his Cinderella.

The pounding in her chest grew stronger. She needed him to kiss her. She needed to see if his lips felt as good against hers as they'd felt on her hand.

"How did I get so lucky?" His voice crooned. Yet

his voice was so soft that it would be impossible for anyone to hear—but her.

If he expected her to speak, he'd be waiting a long time. This whole evening had spiraled beyond anything she ever could have imagined. She was truly speechless, and that didn't happen often.

His head dipped. This was it. He was really going to do it. And she was really going to let him. Her body swayed against his. Her soft curves nestled against his muscular planes.

She lifted on her tiptoes, meeting him halfway. Her eyelids fluttered closed. His smooth lips pressed to hers. At first, neither of them moved. It was as though they were both afraid of where this might lead. But then the chemistry between them swelled, mixed and bubbled up in needy anticipation.

Kyra's arms slid up over his broad shoulders and wrapped around his neck. Her fingers worked their way through the soft, silky strands of his hair. This wasn't so bad. In fact, it was…amazing. Her lips moved of their own accord, opening and welcoming him.

He was delicious, tasting sweet like the bottle of bubbly he'd insisted on ordering. She'd thought it'd just been to celebrate their business arrangement. She had no idea it was part of this seductive proposal. This man was as dangerous to her common sense as he was delicious enough to kiss all night long.

When applause and whistles filled the restaurant, it shattered the illusion. Kyra crashed back to earth and reluctantly pulled back. Her gaze met his passion-filled eyes. He wanted her. That part couldn't be faked. So that kiss had been more than a means to prove to the world that their relationship was real. The kiss had been the heart-pounding, soul-stirring genuine article.

Her shaky fingers moved to her lips. They still tingled. Realizing she was acting like someone who hadn't been kissed before, she moved her hand. Her gaze landed upon her hand and the jaw-dropping rock Cristo had placed there. The large circular diamond had to be at least four, no make that five, carats. It was surrounded by a ring of smaller diamonds. The band was a beautiful rose gold with tiny diamonds adorning the band. She was in love—with the ring, of course.

"Do you like it?" Cristo moved beside her and gazed down at the ring.

"It's simply stunning. But it's far too much."

Cristo leaned over and whispered, "The ring quite suits you even if it can't compare to your beauty. How about we take our cupcake upstairs?"

CHAPTER FOUR

KYRA'S HEART BEAT out a rapid *tap-tap-tap.*

Why was Cristo staring at her as though she was the dessert?

He leaned close and spoke softly. "You're enjoying the evening, aren't you?"

The wispy feel of his hot breath on her neck sent a wave of goose bumps cascading down her arms. "I...I am. It's magical."

"Good. It's not over yet."

This evening had been so romantic that she couldn't help but wonder if he'd almost gotten caught up in the show. Would he kiss her again? Her gaze shifted to his most tempting lips. Did she want him to?

He extended his arm to her and she accepted the gesture. Before they exited the restaurant, she glanced back at the table to make sure she hadn't forgotten anything. "What about the cupcake?"

"It'll be delivered to our suite along with another bottle of champagne." He turned to the waiter to make the arrangements.

Our suite. It sounded so strange. She wasn't sure how she felt about being intimately linked with Cristo—even if it was all a show.

On their way to the elevator, people stopped to congratulate them. Kyra smiled and thanked them, but inside she felt like such a fraud. A liar. Once again her life had become full of lies and innuendos, but this time instead of being a casual observer of her mother's charade, Kyra was the prime star. She didn't like it...but then again, she glanced at Cristo, there were some wonderful benefits. Not that she was confusing fiction with fact, but there was this tiny moment of *what-if* that came over her.

Once inside the elevator, it was just the two of them. He pressed the button for the top floor and swiped his keycard. She knew this was the end of her fairy-tale evening. She needed to get control of her meandering thoughts. It'd help if he wasn't touching her, making her pulse do frantic things. When she tried to withdraw her hand, he placed his other hand over hers.

What in the world?

She turned a questioning glance his way only to find desire reflected in his eyes. Her heart slammed into her chest. Had he forgotten the show was over? They were alone now. But he continued to gaze deep into her eyes, turning her knees to gelatin.

Was it possible he intended to follow up that kiss in the restaurant with another one? Blood pounded in her ears. Was it wrong that she wanted him to do it—to press his mouth to hers? The breath caught in her lungs. She tilted her chin higher. *Do it. I dare you.*

He turned and faced forward. *Wait. What happened?* Had she misread him? She inwardly groaned. This arrangement was going to be so much harder than she ever imagined.

The elevator doors slid open. Another couple waited outside. The young woman was wrapped in her lover's arms. They were kissing and oblivious to everything around them. Caught up in their own world, the elevator doors closed without them noticing. Now, that was love.

It definitely wasn't what had been going on between her and Cristo. That had been—what—lust? Curiosity? Whatever it was, it wasn't real. And now it was over.

Cristo grew increasingly quiet as he escorted her to their suite. He opened the door for her—forever the gentleman. It'd be so much easier to keep her distance from him if he'd just act like one of the self-centered, self-important jerks that her mother insisted on setting her up with because they had a little bit of money and prestige. Her mother never understood those things weren't important to Kyra.

She stopped next to one of the couches and turned back to him. "Thank you for such a wonderful evening." Before she forgot, she slipped the diamond ring from her finger and held it out to him. "Here.

You'd better take this. I don't want anything to happen to it."

He shook his head. "No. It's yours."

"But I can't keep it. It's much too valuable." And held far too many innuendos of love and forever. Things that didn't apply to them.

Cristo frowned. "Now, how would it look if my fiancée went around without a ring on her finger?"

"You're serious? You really want me to wear this? What if something happens to it?"

"Yes, I'm serious. And nothing will happen to it. Besides, I like the way it looks on your hand." He slipped his phone from his pocket and started to flip through messages. "Now, if you'll excuse me, I've got some business to attend to."

"Now? But it's getting late."

His forehead wrinkled as though he was already deep in thought. "It's never too late for work."

And just like that, her carriage turned back into a pumpkin—her prince was more interested in his phone than in her. She felt so foolish for getting caught up in the illusion. Why did she think he'd be any different from the other guys in suits that she'd dated?

"No problem. I'll just go to my room."

There was a knock at the door.

Cristo moved to the door and swung it open. "You're just in time. We were getting thirsty." He turned to her with a warm smile. "Darling, dessert is here. Why don't you go get comfortable and I'll bring it in."

A server rolled in a cart with a cupcake tree and a bottle of bubbly on ice. The man sent her a big smile as though he knew what she would be up to that evening. Wouldn't he be surprised to know that she was going to bed alone?

Kyra was more than happy to head toward the bedroom. Her strides were short but quick. The evening's show had left her emotionally and physically drained. All she wanted to do now was slip into something comfortable and curl up in bed.

"Kyra, you can come back." Cristo turned to her. "Would you like me to open the wine for you?"

She didn't want to return to the living room. And she certainly didn't need any more bubbly. She needed time to sort her thoughts. But on second thought, it was better she went to him rather than having him seek her out.

Reluctantly she strolled back into the living room. "I think I'll turn in early tonight."

"It's probably a good idea. You have a lot to do tomorrow. Good night." He moved to the study just off the living room and pushed the door closed behind him.

How could he turn the charm off and on so casually?

With a sigh, Kyra headed for her bedroom, which was situated across the hall from his. This hotel suite was quite spacious, resembling a penthouse apartment. She should really snap some pictures to show her mother, but Kyra's heart just wasn't in it. Maybe tomorrow.

Her phone chimed with a new message. Still in her fancy dress, she flounced down on the bed with her phone in hand.

MaidintheShade347 (Sofia): Don't keep me hanging. How'd the date go???

Kyra stared at the glowing screen, wondering what in the world to tell her friend. That the night was amazing, magical, romantic…or the truth, it was a mistake. Plain and simple. She shouldn't have agreed to this arrangement. She wasn't an actress. It was just too hard putting on a show. And worst of all, she was getting caught up in her own performance.

Still, she had to respond to Sofia. Her mind raced while her fingers hovered over the screen.

Mop&Glow007 (Kyra): It was nice.

Immediately a message pinged back as though Sofia had been sitting there waiting to hear a detailed report.

MaidintheShade347 (Sofia): Nice? Was it that bad?

Mop&Glow007 (Kyra): It was better than nice.

MaidintheShade347 (Sofia): That's more like. Now spill.

Mop&Glow007 (Kyra): I wore the most amazing dress. We dined downstairs in the High Tide Restaurant.

MaidintheShade347 (Sofia): Good start. So why are you messaging me?

Mop&Glow007 (Kyra): Why not? You messaged me first.

MaidintheShade347 (Sofia): And I'm not with a hot guy.

Mop&Glow007 (Kyra): Neither am I.

MaidintheShade347 (Sofia): You mean the evening is over already?

Mop&Glow007 (Kyra): He's working.

MaidintheShade347 (Sofia): What did you do wrong?

Her? Why did she have to do something wrong? It's not as if they had gone out tonight with romance in mind. The night ended just the way she expected—though she really had thought at some point over dinner that he was truly into her. The man had given an Oscar-winning performance.

Mop&Glow007 (Kyra): I've got a headache. I'm calling it a night. Talk tomorrow.

She kicked off her shoes and stretched her toes. It'd been a long time since she'd spent an evening in heels. She thought she'd left this kind of life back in New York.

Something told her that sleep would be a long way off. She had too much on her mind—a man with unforgettable blue eyes and a laugh that warmed her insides. How in the world was she going to stay focused on finding her family when Cristo was pulling her into his arms and passionately kissing her?

Where was she?

Cristo refilled his coffee mug for the third time that morning and took a long slow sip of the strong brew. He stared across the spacious living room toward the short hallway leading to Kyra's bedroom. Maybe he should go check on her. He started in that direction when her door swung open. He quickly retreated back to the bar, where he made a point of topping off his coffee.

Kyra leisurely strolled into the living room wearing a neon pink, lime green and black tank top. His gaze drifted down to find a pair of black running shorts that showed off her toned legs. Maybe he should have chosen someone who was less distracting to play the part of his fiancée.

When he realized he was staring, he moved his gaze back to her face. "Good morning."

"Morning." She stretched, revealing the flesh of her flat stomach. Cristo swallowed hard. She yawned and then sent him a sheepish look. Her gaze swept over him from head to foot and then back again. "How long have you been awake?"

He glanced at his watch, finding it was a couple of minutes past seven. "A couple of hours."

Her beautiful eyes widened. "You certainly don't believe in sleeping in, do you?"

He shook his head. "Not when there's work to be done. Would you like some coffee?"

"I'd love some."

He grabbed another mug. "Do you take cream and sugar?"

"Just a couple packs of sweetener."

"Which color do you prefer? Pink? Blue? Yellow?"

"Yellow."

He added the sweetener and gave it a swirl. "If you want to make another pot of coffee, you'll find all of the supplies in the cabinet." He gestured below the coffeemaker. "Make yourself at home."

"You won't be here today?"

He handed over the cup. "I have some meetings in the city that I need to attend. Besides, you'll be so busy that you'll never notice my absence."

"Busy? Doing what?"

"You haven't changed your mind about our arrangement, have you?" He noticed how she fidgeted with the ring on her finger. He hadn't been lying last night when he said it looked perfect on her. In fact, if he hadn't made a hasty exit last night, he would have followed up their kiss with so much more than either of them was ready for at this juncture.

"No. I…I haven't changed my mind."

"Good. Because we made the paper." He grabbed the newspaper from the end of the bar and handed it to her.

"We did. But how?" When she turned to the society page, she gasped.

He had to admit that he'd been a bit shocked when he'd seen the picture of them in a steamy lip-lock. He'd meant for it to look real, but he never imagined it'd be quite so steamy. Had she really melted into his arms so easily—so willingly?

And for a moment, he'd forgotten that it was all pretend. He'd wanted her so much when they'd returned to the suite that it was all he could do to keep his hands to himself. Thank goodness he had the handy excuse of work waiting for him, because a few more minutes around her and his good intentions might have failed him.

"I didn't realize it'd be in the papers." Kyra tossed aside the paper. "This wasn't part of our agreement. This is awful. My mother isn't going to understand. She…she's going to think we're really a couple. That you and I— That we're actually going to get married.

This is a mess. What am I going to tell her? How do I explain this?"

"Calm down. You don't have to tell her anything—"

"Of course I do. When she sees that photo, she'll jump to the obvious conclusion. She'll tell all of her friends. It'll be a nightmare to straighten out."

"No, it won't. Trust me." His soft tones eased her rising anxiety.

"Why should I trust you?"

"Because I made sure this photo was just for the papers here in Athens. Nothing will be printed in New York."

Her gaze narrowed in on him. "Are you absolutely certain?"

He nodded. "I am. Trust me. I have this planned out. We may not be on the front page, but we did make a big headline in the society section. Hopefully it'll be enough to garner Stravos's attention."

"Why would you think this man would look at the society section? Isn't that geared more toward women?"

"Trust me. Nothing gets past this man, especially when he's considering doing business with a person. I'm sure he doesn't stay on top of everything himself, but he has plenty of money to pay people to do the research. But since Stravos is a bit of a hermit living here in Greece on an isolated estate, there's no need for our engagement to be announced in the American papers."

"You're sure?"

"I am."

The rigid line of her shoulders eased and she dropped down on the arm of a couch. "The next time, you might want to mention that part first."

"Would it really be so bad if your mother thought you and I were a couple?"

Kyra immediately nodded. "You have no idea how bad it would be. Until recently, my mother had made it her life's mission to marry me off to one of her friends' sons."

"And you're opposed to getting married?"

"No." Her voice took on a resolute tone. "What I'm opposed to is being someone's arm decoration. I don't want to be someone they drag out for appearances and then forget about the rest of the time."

"I can't believe a man could forget about you."

There was a distinct pause. "It's not worth talking about."

She was one of those women Cristo tried to avoid—the ones who didn't understand the importance of business. He didn't want someone dictating to him when he could and couldn't work. His email constantly needed attention. Almost every bit of correspondence was marked urgent. He didn't want to have to choose between his work and a significant other. Because in the end, his work would win. Work was what he could count on—it wouldn't let him down.

And he didn't imagine there was a man alive who could ignore Kyra. Himself included. He didn't think it was humanly possible. Her presence dominated a room with her beauty and elegance. Even he had gotten carried away the prior evening.

If he was honest with himself, the reason he avoided a serious relationship was because he could never live up to certain expectations. He'd promised himself years ago that he'd never become a father. He'd learned firsthand how precious and fleeting life could be. All it took was one flawed decision, one moment of distraction, and then tragedy strikes.

The dark memories started to crowd in, but Cristo willed them away. He wasn't going to get caught up in the past and the weighty guilt—not now.

Kyra sighed. "My father was a workaholic. He loved us, but I think he loved his work more. My mother would never admit that. For her, he was the love of her life. But I sometimes wonder if she realizes all she missed out on."

"So you want someone who is the exact opposite of your father?" Cristo wasn't quite sure how that would work. What sort of man didn't get caught up in his work?

She shrugged. "Let's just say I'm not interested in getting involved with anyone at this point in my life. But if I were, I'd want to come first. When we're out to dinner, I'd want his attention focused on me and our conversation, not on his phone."

"That sounds fair." He wondered if she was recalling their dinner the prior evening. His full attention had been on her. He wanted to convince himself that it was because he needed to put on a believable show for the public—a besotted lover and all that it entailed. But the truth was the more Kyra had talked, the more captivated he'd become with her. He swallowed hard, stifling his troubling thoughts. "I've left you some information to get you started with the wedding plans. There's every bridal magazine available, the phone numbers of all the local shopkeepers and a credit card to make whatever purchases are necessary."

"You don't mind if I go for a quick run before I start, do you?"

He glanced at her formfitting outfit. It looked good on her. Really good. "Make your own schedule. But just so you know, the wedding is in six weeks. You don't have a lot of time to spare."

"Six weeks?" Her brown eyes opened wide. "You sure don't give a girl much time to plan. It's a good thing this wedding isn't really going to take place. I'm not sure I could work out all of the details in time."

"But you must. There can't be any cutting corners. Nothing that gives the slightest hint this wedding is anything other than genuine."

"I'll try my best." She frowned as she made her way over to the desk to examine the aforementioned items. "How will I know what to spend? Is there a budget?"

"No budget. Use your best judgment. But remember, this wedding is meant to impress important people. Spare no expense in planning our lavish, yet intimate nuptials."

"This is all still pretend, right? You aren't actually planning to go through with the wedding, are you?"

"Of course not."

She sent him a hesitant look as though trying to figure out if he was on the level or not. "I'll do my best. I don't have much experience with wedding planning."

"I'm sure you'll do fine." He grabbed his briefcase and headed for the door, knowing he had lingered longer than was wise. He paused and glanced over his shoulder. "My cell number is on the desk. If you need me, feel free to call. Otherwise, I'll see you for dinner."

"Not so fast. We aren't finished."

CHAPTER FIVE

CRISTO STOPPED IN his tracks.

What could he have forgotten? He thought he'd accounted for everything.

He turned back to Kyra. "Is there something else you need?"

She nodded. "We had an agreement. You said you would help me search for my extended family."

And so he had. But the last thing he had time for at this critical juncture was to go climbing through Kyra's family tree. "Have you tried doing some research online?"

"Yes. But I couldn't figure out how to narrow my search. I thought a trip to a library or somewhere with records of past residents of the area would be helpful."

"Your family, they're from Athens?"

"I'm not sure. I know my grandparents set sail for the States from here."

A frown pulled at his lips. He didn't have time to waste running around on some genealogy project when he had a billion-dollar deal to secure. He'd risked everything on this venture…from his position as CEO of Glamour Hotel and Casino to his tenuous relationship with his father.

Cristo clearly remembered how his father had scoffed at the idea of taking the already successful hotel and casino chain and making it global. Cristo knew if the chain was allowed to become static, that its visitors would find the hotels limited and stale. The Glamour chain would ultimately begin to die off. He refused to let that happen.

Cristo adjusted his grip on his briefcase. "I'll have a car at your disposal. Feel free to visit any of the local villages or the library in Athens."

She pressed her hands to her hips. "I thought you'd be accompanying me. You know, to help search for my family."

He recalled saying something along those lines, but he just didn't have time today. "Sorry. I've got a meeting in the city with a banker."

"And tomorrow?"

Tomorrow he had more meetings planned. He couldn't even get away from the demands on his time in this fake relationship. It just made him all the more determined to retain his independence.

"Cristo?"

"Fine. I'll check my calendar and get back to you after today's meeting."

She nodded.

Before he walked away, he might as well find out what this venture would entail. "What information do you have to go on?" His phone buzzed. "Hold on." He checked the screen. "My car is here. I must go. I'll look at what you have this evening."

As he rushed out the door, his thoughts circled back around to the sight of Kyra in those black shorts that showed off her tanned legs. Even her toenails had been painted a sparkly pink. And then there was that snug tank top that showed off her curves.

His footsteps hesitated. Maybe he should have offered to go running with her. Almost as soon as the thought crossed his mind, he inwardly groaned. He couldn't—he wouldn't—let his beautiful new fiancée distract him from achieving his goal.

He was so close to forging a deal to purchase the Stravos Star Hotels. It was just a matter of time until he heard back from Nikolaos Stravos about that invitation Cristo had extended for a business meeting. That steamy kiss in the newspaper, with the headline of Cristo Kiriakas is Off the Market, should have done the trick.

Her lungs strained.

Her muscles burned.

At last Kyra stopped running. Each breath came in rapid succession.

She leaned back against the stone wall lining the walkway in front of the resort. She knew she should have run first thing that morning instead of putting it off. But she'd become so engrossed with the wedding magazines that she'd found herself flipping through one glossy page after the next. When she got to the tuxes, she imagined Cristo in each of them. The man was so handsome that he would look good in most anything. She wasn't quite so fortunate with her broad hips and short legs. It took a certain kind of dress to hide her imperfections.

By late that afternoon, she'd felt pent-up and her head ached. She had more questions about the wedding than answers. What she needed was to talk with Cristo. She knew the wedding would never actually take place, but he'd insisted they were going for authenticity and to pull that off she needed some answers.

When she made her way back to the suite, she called out to him, "Cristo? Cristo, are you here?"

There wasn't a sound. *Drat.*

She moved to the bar where he'd left her his cell number. She entered it in her phone in order to send him a text message.

Mop&Glow007 (Kyra): I have some questions about the wedding. Will you be home soon?

She figured it wouldn't be too long before he responded as he seemed to have his phone glued to his palm. She imagined him falling asleep with it in his hands. Then again, she could easily imagine something else in his hands…um, make that someone else in his very capable hands. And this time, they wouldn't be putting on a show.

She jerked her thoughts to a halt. She was already hot and sweaty from her run. No need to further torture herself.

Her phone chimed.

CristoKiriakasCEO: Meeting has turned into dinner. Will be late. Don't wait up.

Just like that she'd been dismissed. Forgotten. Frustration bubbled in her veins. Cristo was just like the other men her mother had paraded through her life.

Mop&Glow007 (Kyra): Don't worry. I won't.

Her finger hovered over the send button. But then she realized she was being childish. It wasn't as if they were a real couple. This was all make-believe, thankfully. Her heart went out to any poor woman who actually fell for Cristo's stunning good looks and charming smile. He would forget her, too.

Kyra deleted her heated comment and instead wrote, Have a good night.

She told herself she should be happy. It'd give her quiet time to study for her hotel management accreditation. She hated to admit it, but she was woefully behind. Getting ready to move across the Atlantic had been her priority and then she'd been focused on learning her new position at the Blue Tide Resort.

After a quick shower, she made herself comfortable on the couch. Her assignment was to read four chapters and then complete the online questions.

Before she had time to do more than read one chapter, her phone chimed. Was it Cristo? Kyra anxiously searched the couch for her misplaced phone. Had he had a change of heart? Was he in fact different than the men she'd known? He certainly kept her guessing.

MaidintheShade347 (Sofia): What are you doing?

A wave of disappointment washed over Kyra. She had to quit thinking Cristo would surprise her by being anything other than a workaholic. Soon their arrangement would be over and she could get on with her own life.

Mop&Glow007 (Kyra): Studying.

MaidintheShade347 (Sofia): What? You land a really hot, really rich guy and you're studying???

Mop&Glow007 (Kyra): Cristo isn't here.

MaidintheShade347 (Sofia): He bailed on you for dinner?

So Kyra wasn't the only one with that thought.

Mop&Glow007 (Kyra): His meeting ran late. He won't be back for hours.

MaidintheShade347 (Sofia): Oh, good. My date bailed on me. I'll be right over.

Kyra glanced at the unread material on her e-reader and then back at her phone. Maybe some company was exactly what she needed. It'd help get her head screwed on straight. She'd study later. Satisfied Sofia would put normalcy back into her life, Kyra smiled.

Mop&Glow007 (Kyra): See you soon.

And Sofia wasn't kidding. Within a few minutes, there was a knock at the door. At last the evening was starting to look up. She rushed to the door.

Sofia was a couple of inches shorter than her and wore her dark hair in a pixie cut, which worked well with her heart-shaped face. She strolled into the living room and gazed all around. "So this is your," she said, using air quotes for the next word, "'boyfriend's' place?"

Kyra nodded. "I told you he's rich."

"You didn't say *how* rich. This place is really decked out. It's fancier than those exclusive bungalows I clean." Sofia stopped next to one of the couches and glanced down. "Hey, what's this?"

Oh, shoot. Kyra had totally forgotten to put the bridal magazines away. Now she had a lot of explaining to do.

"Are these yours?" Sofia's puzzled gaze met hers. When Kyra nodded, Sofia asked, "But I thought you were paid to be his girlfriend? You didn't mention anything about marrying him. I would have remembered that."

"I'm not marrying him."

Sofia glanced at the open magazine on the glass coffee table. "Looks like you are to me."

"Well, I'm not. I…I'm planning a wedding."

"For whom?"

"Um…so what do you want to eat?" Kyra moved to the desk to retrieve the menus from the drawer. She'd found them earlier at lunchtime. "We could get a pizza."

"Don't go changing the subject. Are you really marrying some guy you hardly know?"

Why did this whole arrangement sound so terribly wrong when Sofia said it? "Hey, I thought you said I should go for it and enjoy an adventure."

"But I didn't say to marry the dude."

Kyra knew she'd promised Cristo that she wouldn't tell anyone about their arrangement, but Sofia wasn't just anyone. Sofia was her best friend. She was the sister Kyra never had. And right now, she needed someone to talk some common sense into her.

"Let me order the pizza and then we'll talk."

"You bet we will." Sofia grabbed the magazine and sank down on the couch. "By the way, do you think they have pizza here?"

Kyra shrugged. "Isn't pizza international cuisine?"

"If it isn't, it should be."

In no time, the concierge had them connected with a nearby pizzeria. As the phone rang, Kyra realized it was very likely that the employees only spoke Greek. This would be a problem as Kyra only knew basic Greek at this point. *Gia sou*—hi. *Nai*—yes. *O'hi*—no. *Efcharistó*—thank you. She knew nothing about how to order a large pepperoni pizza in Greek.

Luckily the person on the other end of the phone spoke English although with a heavy Greek accent. And in turn, Kyra learned that when requesting extra pizza sauce they referred to it as gravy. She tucked that bit of trivia away for future use as she loved pizza.

With food on the way, Kyra had some explaining to do. She inhaled a steadying breath. After starting at the beginning of the story, she ended with, "And now I'm planning a lavish wedding."

"To go with that amazing ring. Let me see it again."

Kyra held out her hand. "Do you think I'm making a big mistake?"

After Sofia got done ogling the rock for the third time, she leaned back. "From what you say, he's been the perfect gentleman." When Kyra confirmed that with a nod, Sofia continued, "And you're doing it to help your mother?"

Kyra nodded again. "I've never heard her so worried. She wanted me to drop everything and go home. I tried repeatedly to explain that I could help her better from here, but I don't think it registered."

"Well, since you're doing it for a good cause, I'd say enjoy your no-strings-attached engagement."

"Will you be my fake maid of honor?"

"Hmm… I've never been asked to be a fake before. I don't know whether to be flattered or insulted."

"Be flattered. After all, I'm only a fake bride and this is a fake wedding."

"True." They both laughed.

"But the planning part is going to be all real."

"You mean he's really going to shell out cash for a wedding that's never going to take place?"

Kyra nodded. "He obviously has more money than anyone should be allowed."

"In that case, I'd be more than willing to take some of it off his hands."

Kyra grabbed one of the magazines and leaned back on the couch. "I don't think that'll happen, but you could help me pick out obscenely expensive dresses, flowers and whatever else goes into a society wedding. I asked Cristo to help me, but he bailed on me for some business dinner tonight."

Sofia shook her head. "What is it with guys and

work?" And then lines of concern creased her face. "Are you sure he's actually at a business meeting?"

"Yes." Cristo might be a lot of things, but she had no reason to doubt his word. She knew Sofia's trust in men was skewed by the lies her ex had fed her while romancing another woman. "Cristo is a good guy even if his sole focus is his work."

"Too bad. He might have made a great catch."

Just then the pizza arrived. The aroma was divine. They also delivered two espressos and some complimentary limoncello. The wood-fired pizza was fresh and the toppings were plentiful and outrageously good. The evening was shaping up to be a great one…despite the fact she'd been stood up by Cristo.

Why exactly was his business so incredibly important to him?

Did he know what he was missing?

CHAPTER SIX

WHERE HAD THE evening gone?

Cristo loosened his tie and unbuttoned his collar. He stepped into the waiting elevator and pressed the button for the top floor of the Blue Tide Resort. All he wanted to do now was see Kyra's smiling face. He checked his watch. It was almost eleven. Something told him that if she had waited up for him, she wouldn't be smiling.

He'd never meant to be out this late, but after the bank he'd had a meeting with one of the suppliers for the Glamour Hotel chain. Their contract was about to expire and both sides were haggling for better terms. In an effort to soothe rising tensions, one of Cristo's business advisers had suggested they all go out for the evening. It was not what Cristo had in mind, but in the end, an evening away from the boardroom had eased tensions all around. Details were settled in a casual atmosphere to everyone's satisfaction and tomorrow the papers would be signed.

He really hoped Kyra would be waiting up for him.

He didn't know why. Perhaps it was just the thought of having someone to unwind with—someone to share the news of his successful evening. Or maybe it was the way Kyra put him at ease as though he could tell her anything.

He slid his keycard through the reader and opened the door. The first thing that greeted him was the peal of female giggles. Giggles? Really?

He stepped into the room and found Kyra sitting on the floor with her back to him. She and another young woman he'd never met were pointing at pictures in a magazine and laughing. Well, it seemed Kyra was quite self-sufficient and capable of making her own entertainment. For a moment, he regretted missing it.

He cleared his throat. "Good evening."

Both women jumped to their feet and turned to him. Their faces still held smiles. The last thing he felt like doing right now was smiling. Yet there was something contagious about the happiness on Kyra's face. It warmed his chest and eased his tired muscles.

"Oops. Is it really that late?" Kyra glanced down at the mess of papers on the floor. "I guess we got caught up with wedding plans."

Cristo's gaze moved to the young woman at her side. "I see you enlisted help."

Kyra smiled and nodded. "I needed someone to help me." The unspoken accusation that he'd bailed on her was quite evident even in his exhausted state.

Thankfully, Kyra didn't appear angry. "So I asked my friend to join me. Cristo, this is Sofia. Sofia, this is Cristo."

"It's nice to meet you, Sofia."

"Nice to meet you, too." Sofia leaned toward Kyra. "Wow. You weren't kidding."

What exactly did that mean? He sent Kyra a puzzled look. Then again, he wasn't sure he wanted to know.

"Don't mind her." Kyra waved off her friend, who was trying to smother a laugh and failing miserably.

Obviously they were very good friends. He didn't know why that should surprise him. Kyra was easy to get along with. That was one of the reasons he'd asked her to work with him to secure this deal with Stravos. He hoped she'd be able to charm Stravos. So far, nothing else had worked. But what Cristo hadn't anticipated was that he would be the one charmed.

He cleared his throat. "I'm sorry. I was held up and couldn't get back sooner." It was the truth, though by the look on Kyra's face, she didn't exactly believe him. "It looks like you two had a good evening."

"We did. Sofia has agreed to be my fake maid of honor for our fake wedding—"

"You told her?" His jaw tensed. What part of don't tell anyone about their arrangement hadn't she understood?

"Um…I did—"

"I think I should go." Sofia grabbed her purse from the couch and moved toward the door. When she got near him, she paused. "Don't worry. Your secret is safe with me."

"Thank you. There's a lot riding on it." He glanced at Sofia, who didn't look as though she trusted him alone with her friend.

The smile faded from Sofia's face. "Kyra and I go way back. There's nothing I wouldn't do for her. Perhaps I should stay."

Did Sofia think he was going to retaliate in an ungentlemanly way? That was not his style. Not now. Not ever. "You don't have to worry. Kyra will be perfectly safe here. I promise."

Sofia gave him one last assessing glance. Then she turned back to Kyra. "Call me if you need anything, anything at all."

"I will. Thanks."

Once Sofia was out the door, Cristo turned back to Kyra. "It seems your friend doesn't trust me."

"Should she?"

"I suppose that's up to you to answer." Okay. So maybe he hadn't taken it well that Kyra had broken her word to him about keeping this deal on the down-low, but he really didn't think he'd done or said anything out of line. Maybe it was the stress of having his whole career on the line combined with the lateness of the hour that had him a bit sensitive. "Don't worry. I hope to have this deal with Stravos concluded soon."

"Does this mean Stravos agreed to a meeting?"

Cristo shook his head. "Not yet. But I hope to hear from him in the near future."

"Will our arrangement be over as soon as you have your meeting?"

Was there a hopeful note in her voice? Was she that anxious to get away from him? He hoped not. He kind of liked having her around. She certainly made his life a lot more interesting. "We'll need to keep up the pretense of being a happy couple until I have a signed agreement."

CHAPTER SEVEN

KYRA YAWNED AND stretched the next morning.

The weekend had finally arrived. After all of the changes and upheaval that week, it was good to have a chance to regroup. After a quick run, she planned to sit down with Cristo and find out exactly what he had in mind for this wedding. She had a few of her own ideas now that she'd looked over the magazines, but she didn't know if they were what he wanted.

With her hair pulled back in a ponytail and dressed in her running clothes, she headed for the living room. When she didn't find Cristo drinking his morning coffee or looking over one of the many newspapers he had delivered to the suite daily, she took a glance in his office. It was empty. In fact, there was no sign of him. Was it possible he'd actually slept in? She couldn't fathom it.

She contemplated knocking on his bedroom door just to check on him when he came strolling in the front door. She spun around, surprised to find him wearing a suit and tie. "Don't you ever take a day off?"

"Why would I do that?" He wore a serious expression.

"All work and no play makes Cristo a dull boy."

He arched a brow. "You think I'm dull?"

"I don't know. Perhaps." She sent him a smile that said she was teasing him. But her comment wasn't all in jest. She found it frustrating the way he worked night and day. And from all appearances, every day of the week. "You do know that it's okay to take some downtime once in a while, don't you?"

His dark brows drew together as though what she said did not compute. "The world doesn't stop just because it's Saturday. You'd be surprised to know of all the business deals that are agreed to on weekends."

She sighed. "Well, what about the work we have to do here?"

His phone buzzed and he held up a finger to indicate he would be with her in a moment. She was seriously tempted to take his phone from him and give him a time-out. She crossed her arms and tapped her foot.

He quickly typed something into his phone before slipping it in his pocket. "Now, what did you need?"

"You."

A broad smile lifted his kissable lips. "Why didn't you say so? If I had known you wanted me, I would have been at your beck and call."

She rolled her eyes. "Does that line really work on the ladies?"

He shrugged. "I don't know. I never tried it."

"Lucky for them. No wonder you were so desperate for a fake bride if that's the best you've got."

"What can I say? I'm not used to picking up women."

She wasn't for a second going to believe he didn't have a social life. No way. Not with his dark, tanned good looks. "So you're saying they pick you up?"

"In a manner of speaking. Would you like to pick me up?"

She shook her head and waved him off. "Not a chance. You've already given me enough headaches with this wedding that you refuse to help me plan."

"I never refused."

"I know. You're just too busy." Her voice grew weary. Cristo needed to realize she wasn't one of his employees to slough tasks off on. They were in this together. Perhaps he just needed to be reminded of what was at stake. "Maybe we should call the whole thing off."

"What? But we can't."

She pressed her hands to her hips. "You're too busy to help me, and from what I can tell, your plan isn't panning out."

"It's working. Remember, our picture was in the paper?"

"From what you're telling me, this Mr. Stravos is very thorough. You don't think he's going to want to see us together—see if we're really a happy couple?"

Cristo shrugged. "How hard can that be? We fooled everyone in the restaurant."

"That was from a distance. What happens when we have to put on a show for someone—someone who is suspicious of us like Mr. Stravos?"

"So what do you have in mind?"

"Stay here today. We can get to know each other better." When his eyes dipped to her lips, her pulse raced. She swallowed hard. "Not like that. I meant talking. If we're going to portray a happy, loving couple, we should know more about each other."

"But my meeting—"

"Can be rescheduled. This was your idea, not mine. I'm just finding ways to make it work. Unless you just want to forget it all—"

"Okay. I get the point." He sighed. "Let me make a phone call."

"And change into some running clothes." Then, realizing that just because he looked like a Greek god didn't mean he exercised, she added, "You do run, don't you?"

He nodded and moved toward the bedroom. The fresh air and sun would do him good. And if she was lucky, it'd erase the frown from his face.

In no time at all, Cristo had changed into a royal blue tank top that showed off his broad shoulders and muscular biceps. Mmm… This man definitely knew his way around a gym. A pair of navy shorts did nothing to hide his well-defined legs.

Cristo didn't say much on their way to the beach.

In fact, he was so quiet she wondered if he was truly upset with her about ruining his plans for the day.

She came to a stop on the running/walking path and turned to him. "If you don't want to do this, I'll understand."

Cristo started to stretch, lifting both arms over his head. "Are you starting to worry that you can't keep up?"

"Are you serious?"

He didn't say anything, but his stare poked and prodded her.

Her pride refused to let her back down. He might look amazing, but since she'd known him, he hadn't run. She, on the other hand, had been running every morning. "I'm not worried at all. We'll see who keeps up with whom."

He smiled confidently.

Once they warmed up, they took off at a healthy pace. Little by little they kept trying to outdo each other. Kyra was used to running solo, so she'd never been challenged this way.

When she started to get winded, she glanced his way. Cristo hadn't even broken a sweat. What was up with that? Shouldn't a man who spends all of his time going from meeting to meeting be tired by now?

As though he sensed her staring at him, he glanced over at her. "I take it I've surprised you."

What did it hurt to be honest? "Well, kinda. It's just that with you working all of the time, um..."

"You thought I'd be out of shape?"

Her face was already warm from the sun and exertion, so she hoped it'd hide her embarrassment. "I know how busy you are—"

He slowed down to a walk. "Between you and me, I do take time out to exercise."

"But when? You're always going from meeting to meeting."

He sent her a smile. "When something is important enough, you make the time. Sometimes I make it to the gym before heading to the office. Other times I do it at lunch. And on the really stressful days, I go in the evening."

Funny how he found exercise important enough to squeeze in, but he didn't seem to have that same philosophy about his social life. "You must really be health conscious."

"I don't know about that. I still enjoy a nice juicy steak. The exercise is more of a stress reliever for me. I played football all through school and always felt better after a strenuous workout. I guess it stuck."

"Football? Here in Greece?"

"No. I grew up in New York City."

"Small world. So did I." Something told her they may have lived in close proximity but they had led very different lives. "Let me guess. You were the quarterback."

He shook his head. "Sorry to disappoint you. I was a wide receiver, much to my father's disappointment."

"Your father wasn't happy that you played football?"

"He was fine with football, but he thought that a Kiriakas should always be the best. In this case, the quarterback and team captain."

"Surely he was…um, is proud of you."

"We should be getting back. I'll race you." When she didn't respond, he added, "I'll give you a head start."

She wasn't too proud to accept his offer because they both knew with his powerful legs that he could easily beat her. "And winner buys lunch."

She took off, all the while thinking about the relationship between Cristo and his father. Her heart swelled with sympathy for the son who failed to live up to his father's expectations. Was that why Cristo seemed to keep to himself?

Minutes later, Kyra and Cristo relaxed at an umbrella-covered table after their race. She'd ended up winning the race. And though she'd teased him about it, she knew he'd let her win. She hated to admit it, but he could easily outrun her. Maybe there was more to Cristo than profit reports and balance sheets after all.

"Looks like you're buying lunch." Cristo's eyes twinkled with mischief.

"So that's why you let me win?"

"Let you?" He shook his head. "I don't throw races. Are you trying to get out of our little wager?" He sent her a teasing smile.

She wished he wouldn't make her pull everything out of him. It'd be so much nicer if they could chat like friends—like her and Sofia. Open, easy and honest. Kyra squeezed the wedge of lemon over her iced tea. "Do you have siblings?"

He nodded. "Three…erm, two older brothers. And you?"

That was a really strange mistake to make. Who forgot the number of brothers they had? His pointed stare reminded her that she still owed him an answer. "I'm an only child. But Sofia is the sister I always wanted."

"Have you known her long?"

"Since junior high. We've been inseparable ever since. She's the yin to my yang. Although lately she's been a bit more yang." When he sent her a puzzled look, she added, "More sunny rather than shady."

He nodded in understanding. "So does that cover everything?"

She arched a brow. "You're kidding me. This isn't an interview. And we've barely scratched the surface of what I'd want to know about my fiancé, but it's at least a start."

"Honestly, there's not that much to know about me."

She eyed him up, surprised to find he was perfectly serious. Well, the guy may be a workaholic but he certainly couldn't be accused of being conceited.

"There's lots to know about you. Like what's your favorite meal?"

He thought for a moment. "I guess surf and turf."

"Who's your favorite musical group?" She'd bet he was a classical fan.

"U2."

Color her surprised. "Coffee or tea?"

"Coffee."

"Sunrise or sunset?

"Sunrise."

"Left or right?"

His brows drew together. "Left or right what?"

"Oops. Preferred side of the bed."

"Left."

Oh, good. She preferred the right. Not that it mattered, since this relationship was an illusion.

"Now it's my turn." Cristo leaned forward, resting his elbows on the table. He launched into his own rapid-fire questions. She played along, enjoying getting to know him better.

"Top or bottom?" His eyes twinkled with devilment.

Oh, no. She wasn't going there with him. "That's nothing you need to know."

"I disagree." His lips lifted into an ornery grin. "Every fiancé should know these things."

Boy, was it getting warm. Kyra resisted the urge to fan herself. The only thing she could think to do now was change the subject. "So why is this deal with Stravos so important to you?"

Cristo sighed as he leaned back in his chair. He took a sip of his iced coffee. "I plan to expand the

Glamour Hotel and Casino chain, which is currently only a North American venture, into a global business. Stravos has an upscale hotel chain that spans the globe. I've heard rumors his grandson is interested in condensing the family's holdings in order to concentrate their funds on expanding their shipping business. This is the prime time to make my interest in the hotel chain known before they publicly announce it's for sale."

He hadn't really answered her question. She still didn't know his driving desire to make his business bigger and better than before. And from what she sensed, it was more than just a strategic business move. But she didn't want to push him too hard now that he was finally opening up to her.

"Now that we've gotten that out of the way, I really should get some work done today." He downed the rest of his drink.

"What about the wedding? Exactly how far do you want me to go with these wedding preparations?"

"The whole way." His chair scraped against the colorful tiles as he prepared to stand.

He wasn't going to get away, not until they got a few things straight. "You know, I didn't sign on to guess my way through this whole wedding. Engaged couples, well, at least the ones I know, make some of the decisions together."

His jaw tensed as a muscle twitched in his cheek. "But I don't know anything about weddings."

"And you think that I do?"

He shrugged. "But you're a woman. Don't all women dream about their weddings?"

"Not this woman. It was never a priority. I figured someday if I met a guy who could make me his top priority, that we'd settle down together. But I'm not getting married just because it's what my mother expects."

"So what you're saying is you wouldn't marry someone like me—at least not willingly."

She paused, not sure if she should speak the truth or not. But then she figured that a man as rich and powerful as Cristo Kiriakas probably didn't have many people in his life who spoke openly and honestly with him. After all, what could it hurt?

She took a deep breath. "No. I wouldn't marry you. You're too wrapped up in your own world. You say the right things, but when it comes time to the follow-through, you fail—"

"That's not fair. You're just judging me on this one occasion, when I have everything riding on this pivotal deal with Stravos. You have no idea what's at stake here."

"I'm sure I don't. But I'm guessing in your world there's always some huge deal to be made or some catastrophe to resolve. Face it, your business is your mistress. You don't have room in your life for another woman."

His mouth opened, then snapped shut. She had him and he knew it. What could he say to the contrary? Absolutely nothing.

His phone buzzed.

She sighed. "Let me guess. You're going to get that when we're at last having an open and honest conversation?"

He pulled the phone from his pocket. "It could be important."

"Do you ever get a phone call that isn't important?"

He didn't answer her as he took the call and moved toward the rail overlooking the beach, most likely to gain some privacy. And yet again, he'd proven to her why staying single was her best option. She didn't like being shoved aside and forgotten.

The truth of the matter was she wasn't suited for this job. She was getting too emotionally invested in a man and a relationship that would soon disappear from her life. But how did she turn off her emotions?

As Cristo's conversation grew lengthy, her patience shrank. She finished her tea and was about to return to the suite for a shower when she noticed Cristo's voice rising. She glanced around finding that most of the nearby tables were vacant.

"You're just worried, because when this deal goes through—and it will—my hotel chain will rival yours."

Kyra couldn't help but be curious as to what had made Cristo lose his cool. He might be a busy man, but he was very good at the art of deflection. He'd even taken her harsh assessment of him as husband material without raising his voice. Who was on the other end of the phone?

"I'm not disloyal to the family. This is business, pure and simple. Something you taught me as a kid."

She shouldn't be sitting here listening. Yet she couldn't move. She was entranced by this new side of Cristo—this vulnerable aspect.

"I'm sorry you feel that way, Father." His whole body noticeably tensed. "Do what you need to do, and I'll do what I need to do."

Sympathy welled up in Kyra. She knew what it was like to disagree with a parent. She did it more than she liked with her mother.

"You know what? You've always been disappointed in me." Cristo jabbed his fingers through his hair as he started to pace. "Why should this be any different?" And with that, Cristo ended the call.

The breath caught in Kyra's throat. There was a line being drawn in the proverbial sand between the two men. And that wasn't good. Not good at all.

Okay, so maybe she'd had a few heated arguments about her mother's meddling, but it had never gotten that harsh. She knew no matter what she did in life that her mother would love her. She didn't have anything to prove to her mother.

So what in the world had happened between Cristo and his father? Was there always such discord between them? Her heart went out to Cristo as he leaned forward on the rail, keeping his back to her. She could only imagine the turmoil churning inside him.

If she'd had any thoughts about backing out of this arrangement, they were gone now. It was bad enough that his father thought he was going to fail, but for her to pull the rug out from under Cristo when he'd been working night and day to make this deal a success would just be too much.

Suddenly, grabbing a shower didn't seem quite so urgent. "Cristo, I was thinking about ordering brunch. That run really worked up an appetite. Want to join me?"

When he turned to her, his face was pale. Lines by his eyes and mouth were more pronounced. It was as though he'd aged five years during that one phone call. She was tempted to go up to him and wrap her arms around him while murmuring that it would all be better soon. But she knew that his wounded ego would rebuff her sympathies.

Cristo returned to the table and sat down. "That was my father." She'd guessed that much by what she'd overheard, but she didn't say anything as she waited and wondered if Cristo would open up to her. He cleared his throat. "He saw the press release of our engagement."

"But I thought you said it wouldn't be in the New York papers."

"It wasn't. My father has his sources. I just didn't know he had me under such tight scrutiny." Cristo rubbed the back of his neck. "He also found out about my plan to buy the Stravos hotels."

"I take it he's not happy about either of your plans." When Cristo shook his head, she added, "I'm so sorry."

Cristo's dark gaze met hers. "What do you have to be sorry about? You had nothing to do with my father."

"I'm just sorry that you had to argue."

Cristo's brows drew together. "I don't need your pity. My father is a hard, cold man. But once this deal is concluded, I'll have an international hotel chain. It'll even top my two brothers' accomplishments. My father will have no choice but to acknowledge my success. He'll have to admit I'm no longer that irresponsible boy who stood by helplessly while… while, oh, never mind. It doesn't matter now."

On the contrary, it mattered a great deal. But she wouldn't push him. As it was, she understood so much more about him and his driving motivation to make this deal a success. She couldn't even imagine how much it must hurt to need to prove your self-worth to a parent. She would do her utmost to help him.

CHAPTER EIGHT

WHAT DID HE know about planning a wedding?

Nothing. Nada. Zip. Zero.

Cristo sat on the floor of the suite with his back propped against the couch. His legs were stretched out in front of him with his ankles crossed. He couldn't remember the last time he'd had such a leisurely Sunday.

He frowned as he gazed at the glossy magazine cover that Kyra had just dropped in his lap. His gaze moved over the cover. *Finding the Perfect Dress.* He kept reading. *Wedding Night Confessions.* He groaned.

"Did you say something?" Kyra rushed over to him with an armload of magazines.

"No." He willed his phone to ring with an emergency or anything he could construe as an emergency, but the darn thing for the first time ever remained silent. He was stuck. He stifled another groan.

She settled next to him. "It helps if you open it. I've marked some pages."

He grudgingly started flipping through the pages. What he wouldn't do now for a quarterly profit report to review or the *Wall Street Journal* to peruse. Instead, he was looking at articles on which shade of nail polish go best with your gown. He turned the page to find *Flowers on a Budget*.

"Isn't it amazing all of the subjects they cover?" Kyra sounded impressed. "I've learned quite a bit from reading these magazines."

"I certainly wouldn't have thought of these things." And that was no lie. His gaze paused on the headline *Making Your Wedding Night Unforgettable*. The title evoked all sorts of tempting images of Kyra in skimpy—no, scratch that. She'd be wearing a classy white nightie that tempted and teased. He closed the magazine.

"Are you sure something isn't bothering you?" She sent him a worried look and shifted uncomfortably.

Yes. Lots. He struggled for a different subject to discuss, something that wouldn't have him imagining her on their wedding night. And then it came to him. "Actually, there's something I've been meaning to mention."

She laid her pen down on a pad of paper as though giving him her full attention. "I'm listening."

He set aside the bridal magazine with its taunting headlines and got to his feet. He retrieved his briefcase from next to the bar and removed a manila folder.

"Between meetings, I was able to pull up some

preliminary information on your surname." He handed it over to her. Their fingers brushed and a wave of need washed over him. His gaze dipped to her lips. He wondered what she'd do if he were to kiss her again, because that one time just wasn't enough. Not even close.

"You did?" Her face beamed with a hopeful smile.

"Don't go getting too excited. As you probably know, it's a popular name. We're going to need more information to narrow it down. Can you remember any details your father told you? Was he born here?"

"He was born in the States. My grandmother was pregnant with him when they crossed the Atlantic."

"Hmm… That eliminates finding a birth record for your father. Did he ever hear any family names?"

She shook her head. "He said his mother didn't talk much about her family. His father told him it was because she was homesick."

"And your grandfather's family?"

"Died in a flu epidemic. He ended up being raised by friends of the family." Kyra worried her bottom lip. "I do have something that might be helpful in my bedroom."

When she went to stand, he put a hand on her shoulder. "Let's not get sidetracked from this wedding stuff. We can go over the stuff about your family tomorrow."

"Oh." Disappointment rang out in her voice.

She held out the folder. "Thanks for these names. I know it'll be like finding a needle in a haystack, but it's a start." Her eyes grew shiny. "Who knows, I might be holding the name of a relative in my hand."

In that moment, he realized just how much this search for her family meant to her. With him being so distant from his own, Kyra's need to reconnect with hers intrigued him.

He cleared his throat. "How about we make a trip into Athens?"

"To do what?"

"I thought we'd visit the library. Hopefully they'll have lots of old documents."

She clasped her hands together and smiled. "You'd do that for me?"

He nodded. "I'd like to see you find your family."

"Really?" The smile slipped from her face. "I mean, up until now you haven't seemed very interested in helping."

He raked his fingers through his hair. How did he explain this to her when he hadn't really delved into his motives? Why exactly had this become so important to him?

Cristo cleared his throat. "I guess I know what it's like to feel alone and isolated." Wait. Was that honestly how he felt? He didn't like digging into emotions, but the captivated look on her face urged him on. "And I know that it's different because my family is alive. I chose to walk away. You never got a choice."

"Thank you for understanding." Her eyes filled with warmth. "You know, it's not too late to change your mind about reconciling with your family. In fact, this wedding is the perfect excuse to ask them to visit."

He shook his head. It wasn't going to happen. "Speaking of the wedding, didn't you have more stuff we need to go over?"

If anyone could help her track down her family, it was Cristo.

The next morning, Kyra awoke before the alarm. As she showered and dressed, thoughts of Cristo circled around in her mind. She had a good feeling about finding her family now that he was on her side. He spoke Greek fluently and could read it. He knew a great many people, including those with the Pappas name. If Cristo could point her in the right direction, she just might meet her distant relatives.

When she rushed into the living room, she found it empty. She made her way to his study. It was empty, too. Was it possible Cristo had slept in? On a Monday—a workday?

Maybe she should check on him. She started toward his room when she noticed a note on the bar. In a very distinctive scrawl with determined strokes, the blocked capital letters were surprisingly legible.

KYRA,
UNEXPECTED PROBLEM AT THE OFFICE NEEDED MY IMMEDIATE ATTENTION. I'LL MAKE IT UP TO YOU. IN THE

MEANTIME, BELOW ARE SOME WEB-
SITES YOU MIGHT WANT TO CHECK.
HOPE THEY ARE HELPFUL.
CRISTO

Frustration bubbled in Kyra's veins. Why had she believed him when he said he'd help her this morning? She clenched her hand, crinkling the paper. She should have known he'd be too busy.

She had to get out of the suite. Otherwise, she just might invest in a gallon of ice cream. That would not help slim her hips. Besides, a run in the fresh air and sunshine would hopefully soothe away her disappointment in finding out that Cristo was just like the other men she'd dated. Why in the world did she let herself imagine he would be any different?

She pushed herself long and hard. An hour or so later, she returned to the suite feeling a bit better. She was determined to find her family, with or without Cristo's help. She'd gotten this far on her own. She could make it the rest of the way.

After showering again, Kyra settled on the couch with her laptop. She smoothed out the note Cristo had left her and input the first web address, which took her to a Greek social site. Thank goodness her computer had the option to translate everything to English.

She didn't know how much time had passed when she heard the door open. With effort, she continued to stare at the monitor. Try as she might, she couldn't think about anything but the sexy man now standing behind her.

"Hello, Kyra." His deep voice washed over her.

"Hi." She stubbornly refused to make this easy for him. He was the one who'd broken their date as though she should totally understand that business trumps all else, all of the time.

He moved to stand at the end of the couch. "Aren't you even going to look at me?"

Was that some sort of challenge? She glanced at him and then turned back to her computer, already forgetting the site she wanted to visit next. "Did you need something?"

"So this is how it's going to be?"

She closed her laptop and turned to him. "What is that supposed to mean?"

"That you're mad because I had work to do."

She hated how he made it seem as if her search to find her family was so unimportant. If only he knew how much her mother needed it—how much she needed it. "It doesn't matter. I did fine on my own."

"You did?" There was genuine enthusiasm in Cristo's voice as he slid off his suit jacket and draped it over the back of a black leather armchair.

She nodded. "I was able to connect with some people online who pointed me toward some helpful information."

"That's great. Were the sites I left you of any help?"

"Yes. Thank you."

Cristo sat down on the couch and rolled up his sleeves. "I know I let you down today, and I'm truly sorry about that." His gaze met hers, making her heart thump. "But I'm here now and I'd like to do what I can to help. And tomorrow we're off to Athens to do research."

She sent him a hesitant look. "You don't have to. I know you have a lot of work to do—"

"And it can wait. I really do want to help. I promise no emergency will hold us up. So is it a plan?"

He'd apologized and it was a soothing balm to her bruised pride. She smiled. "It's a plan."

"Good. Now, why don't I look over what you have so far while you order room service."

That sounded reasonable to her. "I'll be right back." She rushed out of the room, hoping he wouldn't grow frustrated with her lack of documentation. Seconds later, she returned. "Here's everything."

He accepted the black-and-white snapshot of a young couple obviously very much in love. He turned it over to glance at the back before looking at her. His eyes reflected his confusion. "Where are the birth records, marriage certificates or family bible?"

"I...I don't have them. When my mother realized I was going to continue my father's mission, she gave me this photo. Everything else was destroyed in a fire when my father was a kid. That's a picture of my grandparents here in Greece before they moved to the States."

Cristo glanced back at the black-and-white image. "This isn't a lot to go on."

"But it's a start, isn't it?"

He sighed. "I supposed it is. Do you mind if I borrow this?" He hurried to add, "It won't be long. I just want to make a high-quality copy of it."

Her chest tightened. She couldn't stand the thought of losing the only solid link to her past, but as of right now, it was of no help to her. "Go ahead. Do what you need to." Then for her own peace of mind, she asked, "Do you think there are any clues in it?"

He held up the photo. "I'm interested in the background. If we have it enlarged, we might be able to locate where the photo was taken."

"I used a magnifying glass, but I couldn't make out any signs."

"I'm thinking more about the architecture. If it's unique enough, it could point us in the right direction. Now, show me what you came up with online."

Kyra readily opened her laptop, eager to share the tidbits of information. It was a lot like a jigsaw puzzle. She welcomed the help in figuring out how the information fit together and discerning which information didn't belong.

And at last she had Cristo's full attention. Best of all, the more they talked, the more excited he became with the project. He filled her with hope that at last she might find any lingering relatives.

They sat in the living room all evening, scouring the internet and eating room service. Kyra saw a different side of Cristo, a down-to-earth quality. And she liked it. A lot.

Now, how could she get him to let down his guard again? She really enjoyed seeing him smile.

CHAPTER NINE

IT HADN'T WORKED out quite as he'd planned.

Cristo glanced over at Kyra as their limo inched its way through the congested streets of Athens. "I'm sorry our visit to the library wasn't more productive."

"It's not your fault. After all, you helped me search through countless newspapers, journals and books. We may not have uncovered anything, but it wasn't for lack of trying."

He breathed a little easier. "Don't give up. We still have the picture of your grandparents. It's got to have some clues."

She lowered her head and shrugged. "Perhaps."

Even though they weren't able to track down any documents with her grandparents' names, he refused to give up and she couldn't, either. "You know that library is huge. They have thousands of documents. I'm sure we've barely even scratched the surface. We'll just keep at it until we head in the right direction."

"You're right. It's just so frustrating."

"Then think about something else for a while."

"Actually, I do have some questions for you." She withdrew a notebook and pen from her purse. "How many people are you considering inviting to the wedding?"

"You want to do this here? Now?"

"What else do we have to do?"

Some tempting thoughts sprang to mind. "I can think of something a lot more fun."

His gaze moved to the partition that was currently down. If he was to put it up, they'd have all the privacy needed and then he could claim her lips.

A smile tugged at her lips. "That's not what I meant."

"But I promise you'll enjoy it." He playfully reached out for her, but she scooted away. He frowned at her. "Fine. You win. What was it you wanted to know?"

"How big should the wedding be?"

"I'm thinking something small and intimate. Maybe five hundred people."

"Five hundred?" Kyra's mouth gaped. "Are you serious?"

He shrugged. "What were you thinking?"

"Twenty would work for me. But I know you're a very popular person, so how about one hundred people?"

That wasn't many people. There was family, business associates and employees to consider. Still, there was a certain appeal to an intimate gathering. "Considering we'll be having the ceremony here in

Athens rather than in New York, I'm guessing you won't be having many guests."

She shook her head.

Surely he could cut back on the invites. He gave it a bit of thought. "I should be able to get out of inviting a number of people because of the location. It'll take some effort, but I think we can make one hundred people work."

She noted something in her day planner. "I've done some online research and there are invitation addressing and mailing services. I think at this late date it'd be our best option. For a fee, I can put a rush on the order."

"Yes. Yes. The price doesn't matter."

She reached in her purse for an electronic tablet. "What's your favorite color?"

"Why?"

"I need it for the invitations." Her fingers moved rapidly over the screen.

"I guess it's blue." He honestly didn't think anyone had ever asked him that question. "And what's yours?"

"My what?" she asked as though she had been lost in thought.

"Your favorite color?"

"It's aqua." She focused on the tablet and then said, "I've got some invitations picked out. It's just a matter of narrowing them down. Ah, here's one that uses both of our colors. How about a beach-theme invitation with the background being the sand

and water with a blue sky?" She turned the screen around for him to see a picture of the proposed invitation. "And for a fee they can add a gold ribbon and starfish. They'll be sent in little blue boxes."

If she liked it, that was good enough for him. "Go ahead and place the order. And you're sure it'll get to everyone in time?"

She nodded. "As long as you give me those names and addresses today."

He was afraid she'd say that. "I'll list the names and my assistant can give you the addresses."

"You do know that once we send out the invitations your family and friends will know about this thing between us. How are you going to explain the fact they've never met me or even heard of me?"

He hadn't thought of that. "I'll tell them the truth. That we met here at the resort…and it was love at first sight."

"And you think they'll believe it?"

"Most definitely. You're so gorgeous, how could I not be captivated by you?"

"You're making that up."

"I could never make up something like that. Between your beauty and your warm personality, I'm not sure which won me over first."

He wished he was better with words. If he was, he'd tell her how her big brown eyes glittered with specks of gold. They were utterly mesmerizing. Her cheeks held a rosy hue. And her lips…well, they were so sweet and tempting. He knew that for a fact because the kiss they'd shared was forever imprinted upon his mind.

And when he was alone, it wasn't facts and figures that filled his mind these days, it was figuring out how to steal another kiss. Perhaps he could suggest they practice some more, so that it seemed natural when they had to do it in front of people.

He may not be able to articulate how she made him feel, but he could show her. Going with the moment and refusing to consider the implications, he reached his hand out to her. His thumb traced her jaw. "You're the most amazing woman I've ever known."

She continued to stare into his eyes. His heart pounded against his ribs. Did she have any idea what she could do to him with just a look? He should back away.

But he needed to taste her once more. His gaze dipped to her shimmery lips. Instead of the calm, sophisticated businessman that he liked to portray to the world, right now he felt like a nervous teenage boy.

The tug-of-war between right and wrong raged within him. All the while his fingers continued to stroke her smooth skin. His pulse quickened and the pounding of his heart drowned out the voices.

He leaned forward. His lips claimed hers. Gently and hesitantly. He had no idea if she felt the same way.

But then her hands moved over his shoulders and wrapped around his neck. Her mouth moved beneath his. No kiss had ever rocked his world like hers. He didn't know what was so different about her. He just knew he never seemed to get enough.

His phone buzzed and Kyra pulled away.

Of all the lousy times. Cristo swore under his breath. With the moment ruined, he reached for his phone. "Kiriakas here."

"Mr. Cristo Kiriakas?"

"Speaking." He really should have checked the caller ID, because he didn't recognize the female voice.

"I'm calling on behalf of Nikolaos Stravos. He would like to know if you are available for dinner."

She named a date in the coming week. The acceptance teetered on the tip of Cristo's tongue, but he held it back for just a moment—just long enough so this employee of Stravos's didn't know just how anxious he was for this meeting. After a slow, deep breath in and out, Cristo said, "As it happens, I could rearrange my calendar."

"He also requested you bring your fiancée. Would that be possible?"

Cristo's gaze moved to Kyra's beautiful face. "Yes, we will both be able to attend."

"Good." The woman filled him in on the details.

When Cristo disconnected the call, he was a bit stunned. His plan was really working. Okay, so he had had a few doubts along the way. And when his father had insisted he was doomed to fail, his confidence had wavered just a bit. But thanks to Kyra sticking by his side, he'd kept moving forward and it had paid off.

Curiosity glittered in Kyra's eyes. "Well?"

"That was one of Stravos's employees. He wants to have dinner."

"Really?" Kyra clapped her hands tightly together. "This is good, isn't it?"

He nodded.

"Yay! Congratulations." A big grin lit up her entire face.

For a moment, he didn't move. He'd been so stunned by her rush of emotions. He wasn't used to people getting outwardly excited. His family and coworkers were quite reserved. But maybe just this once, it wouldn't hurt to follow her lead. He smiled.

"And it's all thanks to you."

"Me?" She pressed a hand to her chest. "I didn't do anything."

He wasn't going to argue with her, but he couldn't have done any of this without her. And it wasn't just the dinner—she'd gotten him to remember that there was more to life than work. And she'd reminded him how good it felt to smile—really smile, the kind that started on the inside and radiated outward.

Cristo cleared his throat. "Dinner is next weekend."

Her smile turned upside down. "But I have absolutely nothing to wear. I'm presuming this will be a formal affair."

"Yes, it will be. Mr. Stravos is very old-fashioned and quite proper."

"What will you be wearing?"

"A black suit." Then witnessing the mounting stress on her face, he added, "You'll want something stunning. Something that will turn heads."

"Really?"

"Most definitely. I want Stravos to see just how amazing you are. Don't worry. When we get back to the resort, I'll ring downstairs and arrange to have the boutique send up their best dresses for you to choose from."

The worry lines faded from her face. "You'd do that for me?"

There was a whole lot he'd do for her, but he kept it to himself. "Of course. After all, you are doing me the favor."

And with that he made a point of answering emails on his phone. He needed some time to straighten out his jumbled thoughts. Kyra had an effect on him unlike any other. And that wasn't good. He needed to be sharp and focused for his meeting with Stravos.

CHAPTER TEN

THE WEEK HAD flown by what with wedding plans and studying.

At last Friday had arrived as well as Kyra's generous paycheck.

She frowned. *That just can't be right.* She disconnected the phone call with a bank in New York after attempting to make a payment on her mother's mortgage. The problem was the bank didn't want to take her money. They said the mortgage had been paid in full. *How could that be?*

She immediately dialed her mother's number. Maybe her mother had moved the mortgage to another bank. That had to be it, because her mother wouldn't have called the other week panicked if the mortgage had been mysteriously paid off.

"Hi, Kyra." Her mother's pleasant voice sounded so clear that it was as if she was next door, not an ocean away. "I can't talk long. I'm at work. At least I still have one job—"

"Mom, we need to talk."

"Okay. About what?"

"The mortgage."

"Have you changed your mind about coming home? I'm sure between the two of us, we can make the payment."

"Where's the mortgage?"

"What do you mean? It's at the bank, of course."

Something wasn't adding up. "The same bank Dad used?"

"Yes. But you don't need to contact them. I'm taking care of everything. I…I explained that the next payment might be late. They were very understanding."

An understanding bank? The words sounded off-key. In fact, her mother wasn't quite acting like herself.

"Kyra, I need to go. We can talk later."

At last Kyra could no longer deny the truth. Her mother was lying to her. The knowledge sliced into her heart. The one person she was supposed to be able to blindly trust was capable of deceit. But why?

"Mom! Stop! I know the truth."

"What truth? I don't know what you're talking about." Her mother's voice was unusually high-pitched.

"I just called the bank. They told me the mortgage has been paid in full for the past year since… since Dad died. How could you do it?" A rush of emotions had Kyra blinking repeatedly. "How could you let me believe Dad had let us down—that he left us in debt?"

"Kyra, you have to understand. I did it all for you—"

"Me? No. You did it for yourself. You lied and connived so you could control me."

"You're wrong! You don't understand. I couldn't lose you, too. We need each other."

"Not anymore." Kyra pressed the end button on her phone.

In a matter of minutes, everything she thought she knew about her life and her family had come undone. She swiped away a tear as it streaked down her face. How could her mother let her think the worst of her father—that he was irresponsible and careless? None of it was true. Her father wasn't perfect, but he had taken care of them.

The walls were closing in.

Kyra paced back and forth in the suite. Her thoughts raced until her head started to pound. What she needed was a distraction—something to calm her down. First she phoned Cristo, then she called Sofia. She struck out twice.

Everyone but her had plans on a Friday night. Cristo was away on business. And even Sofia had plans with some friends from the housekeeping department. That left Kyra on her own. And there was no way she was going to thumb through any more bridal magazines, conduct any further internet searches for a clue to her family or study for her online classes.

She opened the French doors leading out to the

private balcony. The moon shone overheard and reflected off the serene cove. She leaned against the rail, enjoying the warmth of the evening air.

How was she ever supposed to trust anyone after this? Her mother had lied to her. And not just a little fib, but an ongoing whopper of a tale. If it hadn't been for her mother, she wouldn't be standing in this extravagant suite pretending to be Cristo's bride. Did her mother have any idea what her lies had done to Kyra's life?

The lapping sound of the cove beckoned to her. It would be just perfect for a nighttime dip. After all, she'd been in Greece for several weeks, and she had yet to stick her toes in the clear, inviting water. Tonight she would remedy that.

Determined to wear off some of her frustration after speaking to her mother, Kyra rushed to her room and slipped on her brand-new turquoise bikini. She scribbled a note for Cristo, just in case he returned sometime that evening and actually noticed her absence. With a white crocheted cover-up and flip-flops, she rushed to the beach.

She discarded her cover-up and towel on the sand. The water was warm and she waded farther in. This would be the perfect way to clear her mind. But even then, thoughts of betrayal ate at her.

Ever since her father died, she had worked so hard to be the perfect daughter, to put her mother's needs first, to play by the rules. But no more. Now she was going to do what she wanted—what made her happy.

Kyra moved farther into the water until it was up to her shoulders. Was it wrong that she sometimes wondered what it would have been like if she and Cristo had met under different circumstances? Would he have asked her out just because he found her attractive or intriguing? She sighed with regret over never knowing the answer.

She fell back in the water and began to float. So far, Cristo had been nothing but a gentleman…when he wasn't working. Which wasn't often. She really wondered if anyone would believe he was madly in love with her. She started to do the backstroke. A few strong strokes and then she coasted.

Thoughts of Cristo crowded her mind. Though he could be sweet and was devastatingly handsome, he didn't have room in his life for a woman because he already had a mistress—his work. And his mistress was demanding—too demanding. Or was he using his work as an excuse to avoid a serious relationship? If so, why?

There was a splash of water behind her. The little hairs on the back of her neck lifted. She wasn't alone. Her gaze sought out the shore. She wasn't far from it, but could she get there before whoever it was caught her?

She started for the shore when a hand reached out and caught her foot. A scream tore from her lungs. She started to struggle, splashing water in her eyes.

"Kyra! It's me. Cristo."

She stopped struggling. "What in the world are you doing? Trying to scare me to death?"

"Sorry. You looked so peaceful floating on the water that I didn't want to ruin the moment."

"Well, you certainly did that. I didn't hear you." And then she caught sight of his muscular chest. Okay, so maybe she wasn't so upset about him joining her. The moon reflected off the droplets of water on his bare flesh, making it quite tempting to reach out and slide her fingertips over his skin. Her fingers tingled at the thought.

"It wasn't my intention to startle you. It's just when I got back to the suite and saw your note, a night swim sounded like a good idea. I thought I'd join you, but if you want me to go, I'll understand."

"No. Stay." She tried to catch a glimpse of what he was wearing, but the water was too dark to make out anything.

So she was left to wonder what sort of swimwear he preferred. Perhaps he was skinny-dipping. Nah, not Cristo. He was too proper. Maybe it was a pair of those itty-bitty bikini bottoms. She immediately rejected the image. Perhaps he wore some shorty-shorts—better yet low-slung board shorts.

Cristo's gaze met hers. "You're sure you want me to stay?"

She nodded, still working up the courage to reach out and run her hands over his chest. "I'm actually happy to see you. I thought you'd be working until late."

"I had something better to do." A mischievous smile lit up his face, making him even more handsome.

Was he flirting with her? It sure sounded like it to her. A smile pulled at her lips. "And what would that be?"

His voice lowered. "Spend time with my fiancée. Didn't you say it was important we learn more about each other?"

"I did. Do you swim much?"

"Wait a sec. This was my idea. I get to ask the first question."

"And what would that be?"

His gaze narrowed. "Have you ever gone skinny-dipping?"

Thankfully the moonlight wasn't that bright, because Kyra was certain her cheeks were bright red. "No."

"Oh, come on," he coaxed. "You can tell me."

"I am. I haven't. But I take it you have."

He nonchalantly shrugged. "I was at boarding school. It was a dare. There was no way I could back out."

She shook her head. "You must have been a handful as a kid."

"And you were a straight-A student and a Goody Two-shoes who did no wrong."

Was she really that predictable? She stuck her

tongue out at him. He let out a deep laugh that made her stomach flip-flop.

Still chuckling, he turned and swam away from the beach. The gentle lap of the water filled the quietness of the evening. No way was he getting away that easily. She followed him.

They paddled around the cove, laughing, playing and enjoying the intimacy of having the water to themselves. Okay, so maybe Cristo wasn't a complete workaholic. Kyra's cheeks began to ache as she continued to smile, but she couldn't help herself. Tonight Cristo was engaging and entertaining. Just what she needed to take her mind off her troubles.

She moved up next to him. "I'm surprised you'd take the evening off to splash around the cove with me."

"What, you thought I'd forgotten how to have a good time?"

She shrugged. "Something like that."

"Well, I'm glad to prove you wrong." He cupped his hands together and sent water splashing in her direction.

She sputtered, caught off guard. She swiped the water from her eyes to find Cristo grinning. No way was she letting him get away with that. She held her arm out at her side and swiped it along the surface of the water, sending a much larger spray in his direction. The next thing she knew they were engaged in a heated water battle until Kyra's arms grew tired and she gave up the victory to him.

"Is my water nymph worn-out?" Cristo moved closer.

"Yes." She leaned her head back, dipping her long hair in the water before smoothing it into place. "Aren't you tired, too?"

"Not too tired to do this." His hands slipped around her waist, pulling her close.

His lips claimed hers. What was up with him? He'd kept his distance from her after the kiss in the limo. Perhaps it had confused him as much as it had her. Whatever it was, she approved.

His mouth moved lightly, tentatively as though testing the waters. Her hands moved to his bare shoulders, enjoying the feel of his muscles beneath her fingertips.

As the kiss deepened, her legs wrapped around his waist. The kiss went on and on. They definitely had this part of their relationship down pat. Then again, maybe a little more practice would be good.

Cristo carried her out of the water. All the while their kiss continued, and Kyra's heart pounded. Could this really be happening? Was she really falling head over heels for this man?

She couldn't think clearly. It was as though the full moon had cast a spell over them—anything seemed possible. And she didn't want this moment to end—not now—not ever.

However, when a breeze rushed over her wet skin, a chill set in. She pulled back. In the moonlight, she stared into Cristo's puzzled gaze.

She attempted to steady her rushed breathing in order to speak. "We can't keep this up. What if someone sees?"

"They'll probably get some ideas of their own." His brows lifted. "You do remember we're supposed to act like we're on a romantic getaway, right? Consider this a dress rehearsal."

His words were like a cold shower. Was that really what he thought they were doing here? Putting on a show? The realization stabbed at her heart. Here she was getting caught up in the moment and he was figuring out how to get the most mileage out of their public display of affection.

She untangled her limbs from him. Goose bumps raced over her flesh, but the heat of her indignation offset the chill of the night air. "It's getting late. We should go inside."

"And continue this?" There was genuine hope in his voice.

"Um…no. I think we have this kissing stuff down pat."

"Are you sure? I'm thinking I might need a little more practice."

"You do remember this is all make-believe, right?" With each passing day, she found it harder and harder to draw the line between their fake engagement and real life. The lines kept blurring and they were starting to fade away.

Cristo sighed. "I remember. And tomorrow night

will be our big test. Do you think we can pull it off?"

"I think we have a good chance. But when we're alone, we can't keep forgetting about the boundaries in this pretend relationship."

Cristo stepped back. "Is that what you really want? Because while we were out in the water, I got the distinct impression you wanted more."

For a while there, she thought she could play the part of girl gone wild. The truth was, while her mother's actions had hurt her deeply, she was still the same person inside, just a bit more scarred.

"I…I didn't mean to lead you on." She glanced away.

He placed a finger beneath her chin and lifted until their gazes met. "Talk to me. You're not acting like yourself. What's going on?"

"It's nothing."

"It's definitely something." His voice was low and soothing. "I'm your friend. I'd like to be there for you. If you'd let me."

She moved to where she'd left her towel and cover-up. Maybe it would help to talk about it. Cristo would know that he wasn't alone with his problems coping with his parents.

As she dried off, she chanced a quick glance over her shoulder in order to satisfy her curiosity. He indeed was wearing a pair of dark board shorts with a white stripe around each leg. In the moonlight, his shorts hung low enough to show off his trim abs. His head lifted and their gazes met. He ran a towel over his chest, but he didn't say a word. It was as though he was waiting for her to start the conversation.

She slipped on her crocheted cover-up. She spread out her towel on the sand and sat down. "Join me."

He did. His shoulder brushed against hers. She ignored the nervous quiver his touch set off in her stomach.

"The reason I agreed to play the part of your fiancée was because it allowed me to help my mother. But today, I learned that everything I believed is… is a lie." She went on to reveal her mother's duplicity. The whole sordid story.

When it was all out there, Cristo draped an arm over her shoulders and pulled her close. She let her head rest against his shoulder, taking comfort in his touch. He didn't have to say a word. There was comfort and understanding in his touch.

She didn't know how much time had passed before they started for their suite. This gentle side of Cristo was even harder for her to resist. But she knew that if she let Cristo get too close, he'd wedge his way into her heart. From that point forward, she would forever be comparing every man she met to Cristo. And she already knew they wouldn't live up to Cristo's larger-than-life personality.

She couldn't let that happen. She had to stay strong for a little longer.

CHAPTER ELEVEN

So this is what it's like to ride in a helicopter.

Kyra gazed out the window as the lights of the Blue Tide faded into the distance. She was never going to forget this experience.

Thankfully she'd had the forethought to document it. She stared down at the new photo on her phone. It was of her and Cristo standing next to the helicopter in their evening clothes. If she didn't know better, they really did look like a genuine couple. Cristo was so sexy in his black suit, black dress shirt and steel-gray tie. Any woman would be out of her mind not to want to be on his arm. She cast Cristo a glance, surprised to see he was staring back at her. Her stomach dipped.

She would have liked to talk to him, but the *whoop-whoop* of the helicopter blades made that difficult. Even the headset Cristo had given her hadn't done much to offset the rumbling sound. She turned to stare out the window. The brilliant rays of pink, orange and purple of the setting sun took her breath away.

She adjusted the beaded, pearl-colored bodice of her strapless dress. Cristo had told her to go with something stunning. She truly hoped this dress was what he'd had in mind. With him being tense over the upcoming dinner, he hadn't seemed to notice her, much less her dress.

Thankfully the saleswoman assured Kyra the dress was made for her. The crystal-beaded bodice led to a beaded waist followed by a hi-low handkerchief skirt of sky blue. She wiggled her freshly pedicured toes in the new silver heels with a rhinestone strap. She couldn't remember the last time she'd been this dolled up.

Kyra glanced over at her dashing escort. She was really hoping he would notice all of her hard work. As though he'd sensed her staring, he glanced her way. Their gazes met. He reached out, taking her hand in his and giving it a reassuring squeeze. His warm touch calmed the fluttering sensation in her stomach. She wanted so desperately to help him today, but she worried whether she'd be able to pull it off.

The helicopter touched down on a fully lit helipad not far from an impressive coastal mansion. The grounds surrounding the white mansion with a red tile roof were illuminated by strategically placed spotlights. Kyra was awed by the enormity of the home.

After Cristo helped her exit the helicopter, she turned to him. "One man lives here? All by himself?"

Cristo's gaze moved to the mansion and then back to her. "His grandson lives with him. And I'm sure there's a household staff."

"I'd get lonely." She turned all around, not finding any signs of neighbors. "This place really is isolated out here on this island."

"Don't worry." Cristo wrapped his arm around her waist and pulled her to his side. He placed a kiss upon the top of her head. His voice lowered. "You're safe with me."

She lifted her chin and gazed into his eyes. She couldn't read his thoughts. But when he ran a finger along her cheek, her heart went *tip-tap-tap* in her chest. Was he being sincere? Or was this just another performance?

"Welcome." A male voice interrupted the moment. "I'm Mr. Stravos's butler."

With great regret, she turned to find an older gentleman standing off to the side of the helipad. Immediately, her heart settled back to its normal pace. So Cristo had seen the man approaching and it had all been a show.

Right now, all she wanted to do was pull away from Cristo. She felt foolish and gullible. But considering their agreement, she was stuck acting as his loving and devoted fiancée. She choked down her disappointment.

Cristo took her hand and placed it in the crook of his arm. They followed the butler to the grand house. The sand and sea were only a few yards away. The lull of the water pounding the rocky cliff filled in the silence. The walkway led them to a portico that stretched the length of the house. Impressive columns were placed every ten feet or so.

At the center of the structure was a courtyard. A wrought-iron gate stood open, welcoming them into the tiled area. A working water fountain stood prominently in the middle highlighted with different colored lights.

Surrounding the fountain sat various groupings of patio furniture, from a wrought-iron picnic table for four to a couple of cushioned loungers. At the far end stood a fireplace. It glowed as a log burned in it. Kyra was awed by the entire courtyard.

A tug on her arm had her realizing they were being led inside. Kyra grudgingly followed along. She had a job to do this evening and she intended to do her best. The sooner Cristo had a signed agreement, the sooner this arrangement between them would end. Cristo would have his precious contract and she'd have her life back.

Though her stomach quivered with nerves, Kyra knew how to do this. At last there was some benefit from the years of witnessing her mother putting on airs for her friends. Kyra knew how to embellish and imply things without outright lying. It was an art of inflection and knowing what to leave out. Her mother was an expert, and it'd only gotten worse since the death of Kyra's father. Kyra shoved the troubling thought to the back of her mind. Right now, she had a job to do.

The living room was quite formal with two full-length white couches facing each other. There were four wing-backed chairs in burgundy upholstery. At the far end of the room was a prominent stone fireplace. On the perimeter were various types of artwork from a bust of some Greek hero to paintings of historical figures and the Greek ruins.

When Kyra went to free her hand from Cristo's in order to further explore her surroundings, he tightened his grip. What in the world? Was he worried that she'd slip away and leave him on his own?

"Welcome." Another man entered the room. He approached them and smiled. But she noticed immediately that his smile didn't quite reach his eyes. "I'm Nikolaos Stravos III, but please call me Niko."

The man was approximately Cristo's age. Niko was handsome in a tall and dark kind of way. But in Kyra's mind, he didn't hold a candle to Cristo. And it was then she realized she was starting to measure other men according to Cristo's yardstick. Not good. Not good at all.

She tried to see Niko clearly without the comparison to the larger-than-life man at her side. Niko had dark wavy hair, which was finger-combed back off his face. It was a very relaxed look for a man whose grandfather seemed so old-fashioned. Or maybe that was why Niko had a casual appearance—it was opposite of what his grandfather would want. The fact he would stand up to the senior Stravos instead of catering to the older man scored him a few points in Kyra's book.

Cristo shook his hand and introduced himself before turning to her. "And this is my fiancée, Kyra Pappas."

She presented what she hoped was a bright and friendly smile. "I'm pleased to meet you."

Cristo cleared his throat. "Will your grandfather be able to join us this evening?"

Niko's face creased with lines. "I hope you won't be too upset to learn that I'm the one who invited you here."

"You? But why?" It wasn't Cristo who spoke those words but rather Kyra. And it wasn't until the words were out there, followed by an awkward silence, that she realized she shouldn't have spoken so freely. The heat of embarrassment rose up her neck as both men cast her raised brows.

Niko lifted his chiseled chin as he faced Cristo again. "As I was saying, my grandfather is quite set in his ways and I've been trying to talk him into making some changes."

Cristo sent her a warning look not to say anything else. He turned back to their host. "And you are the one considering selling off the hotel chain?"

"How about we dine first? Everything is ready now."

"And your grandfather? Will he be joining us later?"

"He has a lot of work to deal with. But I mentioned the dinner to him earlier today." Niko waved the way to the dining room.

At least food would give her something to do, since talking hadn't gone so well for her. Not a great way to start the evening. The problem was her nervousness. Cristo's tension had rubbed off on her and now she had to relax if she wanted to help her fiancé.

Why had Stravos's grandson requested this meeting?

Cristo attempted to keep up the light conversation about football. All the while, he kept wondering if there'd been a shift in power in the Stravos organization. But how would his investigators have missed such huge news? The answer was they wouldn't have.

Though the dinner itself was quite a delicious affair, Cristo had a hard time enjoying it. He hadn't come here for good food and company. He'd wanted to negotiate a deal or, at a bare minimum, find out what it'd take to strike a deal with Stravos. So far, he knew no more than when he'd arrived at the estate.

"Thank you for the delicious dinner." Kyra folded her linen napkin and set it aside.

"It was my pleasure." Niko pushed back his chair. "I thought we would have dessert out in the courtyard."

"That would be wonderful. I just love what you've done with it." Kyra continued to chatter on about nothing specific, just making idle conversation to fill in the empty spots in the conversation—empty spots left by Cristo's prolonged silence.

He knew he should be friendlier. But he also knew the grandson didn't possess the control needed to make this venture a reality. Right now, he was left hoping for a miracle.

They made their way to the courtyard. Niko turned back to him. "Would you care for some more coffee?"

When Cristo declined, Niko moved to the wrought-iron table with a glass top that held a tray with a coffee carafe as well as cream and sugar. Once his cup was filled, he took a seat in the chair opposite Cristo.

Now that dinner was over and they'd made idle chitchat, it was time to get to the point of this get-together. "I hate to ruin this lovely evening with talk of business, but I was wondering what your thoughts are regarding the sale of the Stravos Star Hotels."

"I've given the subject of selling off the chain considerable thought. My question for you is, why are you so interested in the purchase when you already have a hotel chain of your own?"

"The Glamour Hotel and Casino chain is a North American venture. What I'd like to see happen is to merge the two chains and give the discriminating traveler the global availability of staying with a chain they are comfortable with—that keeps track of their preferences in our universal concierge system. That way, no matter which location they stay in, they'll feel like they're at home."

Niko's eyes lit up. "I take it you have already implemented this feature in your existing hotels?"

"We have, and it has created a large increase in return clientele. You don't have to worry about the Stravos Star Hotels. Though the name will change, the quality will remain exemplary."

They continued into a more detailed discussion of what each of them would like to see take place with the sale. For the most part, there was mutual agreement. There were other areas that were a bit sticky, but Cristo didn't see them as insurmountable hurdles. No deal was ever achieved without its share of negotiating.

Niko set aside his now-empty coffee cup. "I know that if the time comes, our assistants and attorneys can hash through all of this, presenting us with long, dry memos, but I suppose I'm more like my grandfather than I care to admit. I like to be personally involved when it comes to the decisions that will change the course of Stravos Holdings."

"I can appreciate the personal touch. My father is the opposite. He would rather sit in his ivory tower and read reports."

"What a shame to spend so much time locked away in an office." Kyra's eyes pleaded with him to follow her conversation. "I'd love to hear what it's like to live out here on this private island."

"It's quiet." Niko smiled as he settled back in his chair.

There was more business he wanted to discuss,

but perhaps Kyra was right. And Niko seemed like a decent man. "I bet there's good fishing."

"I must admit that I'm not much of a fisherman." Niko refilled his coffee before turning to Kyra. "I'm sure you'd grow bored out here."

"Unless I found something to amuse me."

Was she flirting with Niko? Cristo sat up a bit straighter. Her gaze immediately swung around to him.

"I could definitely imagine some leisurely mornings." Did she just smile and wink at him?

As the playful conversation continued, Cristo forgot about his business agenda and enjoyed the moment. Kyra was captivating and could take most mundane subjects, turn them on their heads and find an interesting angle he hadn't thought of before.

There was a natural warmth and friendliness about her that he hadn't experienced with the other women he'd dated. He started to wonder if this was what life would be like with an amazing lady by his side, one who supported and loved him. And then realizing the dangerous direction of his thoughts, he drew them up short.

Much too soon the conversation wound down and everyone got to their feet. Cristo didn't want the evening to end. He hadn't been this relaxed and happy in a long time.

"Thank you so much for having us." Kyra smiled at Niko.

Cristo held out his arm to escort her back to the

helipad. When her hand looped through the crook of his arm, all felt right again. With her by his side, he didn't have to pretend. It felt as though this was how things were meant to be.

They'd just turned for the gate when there was the sound of footsteps behind them. Assuming it was one of the household staff, Cristo kept moving toward the portico.

"Grandfather, come meet our company."

"Very well." There was a gruff tone to the man's voice.

Cristo turned, having absolutely no idea how this initial meeting would go. The one thing he did know through his abundant research was that the senior Nikolaos Stravos was not a social man. The man preferred his privacy, but he loved his grandson above all else. Hopefully Niko would have some sway with the older man.

Cristo's eyes met a slightly hunched man who in his prime would have towered over Cristo. The man's wavy hair was snow-white and his matching beard and mustache were clipped short. On his nose were perched a pair of black-rimmed reading glasses. It appeared he had been hard at work just as his grandson had claimed.

"Grandfather, please meet Cristo Kiriakas."

Cristo stepped forward and held out his hand. "It's good to meet you, sir. I've heard a lot about you."

The man studied him as though trying to decide

if he wanted to shake it or not. At last the man accepted the gesture. His grip was firm and the handshake was brief.

The senior Stravos pulled back but kept his gaze on Cristo. With his arms crossed, he frowned. Cristo did not have a good feeling about this meeting—not good at all. Was the man always this hostile?

"Grandfather, wouldn't you like to meet Kyra—"

"What I'd like is to know why this man has been digging around in my business and my life." The man's voice was deep and rumbled with anger.

"Excuse me?" Cristo feigned innocence while he figured out how best to handle this situation.

"There is no excuse for the level of digging your men have been doing. Did you really think you'd find whatever you were searching for?"

Perhaps Cristo had been a bit zealous with his quest to make this deal a reality.

Before he could find an appropriate response, Kyra stepped forward. "I'm sure Cristo meant no harm. He's from the States and, well, I think we do things differently from how you do them over here."

Senior Stravos cast her a quick glance. "I should say so. We know when not to cross a line. We have respect—manners."

"Cristo does get excited about business. Sometimes he gets wrapped up in a project to the exclusion of everything and everyone."

Why was she making excuses for him? Didn't she

think he could handle this situation on his own? Not that he'd done a good job so far.

"What my fiancée is trying to say is that I like to do my research before I start negotiations. I like to know everything about who I'm about to do business with. I'm sorry if that offended you or if my team overstepped. That was not my intention."

The man's bushy brows drew together. "And what exactly do you think you have to offer me?"

"Money. And lots of it for your hotel chain."

The man's eyes widened. He turned to his grandson. "Did you know about this?"

"I did."

"And I suppose you think it's a good idea."

Niko straightened his shoulders and met the older man's gaze straight on. "You know I do. We've talked about it numerous times."

"But I didn't know you'd gone behind my back to bring in an outsider to try to sway my opinion."

"It's not like that. You knew I was still exploring the idea of selling off the chain and you knew I invited Cristo here for dinner. I asked you repeatedly to join us."

Nikolaos sighed in exasperation. "I told you I was busy. Besides, a dinner won't change my mind about selling."

This was worse than Cristo had been imagining. This man could give his own father lessons in being obstinate. How in the world was Cristo going to sway the older man to reconsider his position?

Obviously money for a billionaire wouldn't be a deciding factor. It had to be something else—something more personal. But what?

CHAPTER TWELVE

KYRA KNEW CRISTO was in trouble.

Everything he'd been working toward was about to go up in flames—if it hadn't already. She wanted to help, but she didn't know how. And she didn't want to make matters worse.

"You have a very beautiful home here." Kyra smiled at the older man, hoping the neutral subject would ease tensions. "Thanks so much for having us. I can't get over how charming your courtyard is. I especially love the flowers."

The man gazed at her for a moment before turning away. But then his gaze came back to her. There was a strange look in his eyes—like one would give to a person they loosely recognized but couldn't quite place. "Are you American?"

"Yes, I am. My family's from New York."

Mr. Stravos moved to stand next to her, blocking Cristo from the conversation. "And you're in Greece on a holiday?"

There was a slight pause as she debated how honest to be with him. When Cristo went to step forward and intervene, Niko shook his head. This was all up to Kyra. She swallowed hard. Honesty was always the best policy. "I actually came to Greece to work."

"Work? You work for Cristo?"

Kyra might not be a high-powered businessman like everyone else in the room, but she wasn't stupid. She knew Mr. Stravos was on a fishing expedition. He wanted to know if she and Cristo were truly an item or if this was just a scam to secure a business deal. "It started that way, but when we met it was love at first sight."

"Hmpf." Mr. Stravos didn't sound impressed. "So you two don't know each other?"

"That's not true." She'd been learning lots about Cristo, but what she didn't know was where things stood between them. Those kisses they'd shared weren't just for show—no matter what Cristo said. There had been red-hot passion in them. And the way Cristo had looked at her the other night beneath the moonlight in the cove had gone beyond putting on a show for others. There had been hunger and need in his eyes. And there was the way he made her heart race, unlike any man she'd ever met. "How much do you have to know about someone to know they are very special?"

The man's bushy brows rose. "I knew my late wife from childhood. It was expected we would marry."

"Ours was a whirlwind courtship. Cristo swept me off my feet. I don't think it matters how long a couple is together. They just know when it's right." None of which was a lie. She truly believed this. She just hadn't met Mr. Right yet. Her gaze moved to Cristo. He certainly made a really good Mr. Right Now.

"Why come to Athens to work? Don't they have work where you come from?"

She decided to turn the question around on him. "Why not come here? Athens is beautiful. It's an adventure."

"And that's it?"

There was one more thing. Why not tell him? It wasn't a secret. And there was the slight chance that Mr. Stravos might know something about her family. "I came here in search of my extended family."

Mr. Stravos's eyes widened. "You have family here?"

"I hope so. My father's side of the family came from Greece."

"What are their names?"

"Pappas. Otis and Althea Pappas. Cristo has been kind enough to offer to help me search for the records."

A frown pulled at the man's face. Without a word, he turned and headed back into the mansion. Oh, no! What had she done wrong? She cast Cristo a questioning glance, but he was staring at the man's retreating back. This wasn't good. Not good at all.

Kyra turned to Niko. "Was it something I said?"

Niko shook his head. "You were fine."

"Then what just happened?"

"I have no idea." Niko shrugged before turning

back to Cristo. "What can I say? My grandfather is always full of surprises. But don't give up. I'll talk to him."

Cristo stuck out his hand. "I'd really appreciate anything you can do."

Kyra cast Cristo a sympathetic look, but he turned away. She understood that he was deeply disappointed, but there had to be another way. Something he hadn't thought of yet.

They started for the gate when Kyra paused. She turned back to catch Niko just before he entered the living room. "Niko, would it be all right if I sent over a wedding invitation for you and your grandfather?"

"That would be quite thoughtful. But I can't promise we'll be able to make it."

"I'll send one anyway," she said and smiled.

She didn't want to push any further. At least it was something. Maybe nothing would come of it. Then again, who knew what the future might hold. She looped her hand through the crook of Cristo's arm, as was becoming natural to her.

So where did they go from here?

She glanced over at Cristo. His handsome face was marred with stress lines. Now wasn't the time to ask him.

Once back at the Blue Tide Resort, they walked along the paved path that led back to the main building. She kept waiting for him to say something—

anything so she knew where things stood. Unable to stand the prolonged silence, she asked, "How do you think the meeting went?"

He sent her an I-don't-believe-you-have-to-ask look. "Obviously not well."

Was she just being overly sensitive or was his grouchiness directed toward her? Surely he didn't think she intentionally messed things up, did he? She would never do that to him.

"I'm sorry I didn't do a better job convincing Mr. Stravos that we're a happy couple. Perhaps it would be best if we just ended this whole arrangement right now."

Cristo stopped walking and sent her a hard stare. "You're quitting?"

"Don't you think it would be best? I was absolutely no help to you at dinner. And there's no need for us to be in each other's way."

"No." His voice held strength and finality to it.

No? What did he mean no? "You aren't even going to consider letting me out of this arrangement?"

He shook his head. "When I make a deal with someone, I expect them to keep up their end of the bargain."

"But I don't understand. Mr. Stravos looked at me as though he didn't believe a word I said—it was as though he could see straight through our story. I think this whole engagement is a huge mistake. I'm sorry I failed you."

"It wasn't you." Cristo reached out, took her hand

in his and squeezed it. "You have nothing to apologize for. You did everything right, and I appreciate it."

She stared straight into his eyes, trying to determine the depth of his sincerity. "You really mean that? You're not just saying it to make me feel better?"

"Trust me. I mean every word." He shifted his weight from one foot to the other. "If anything, this is all my fault for thinking up such a far-fetched scheme."

"There has to be another way to convince the elder Stravos that the sale is good for everyone. After all, his grandson is all for the deal."

"The problem is I'm running out of ideas." There was a worrisome tone in his voice—one she'd never heard before.

She realized that she'd come to care for Cristo far more than she ever imagined possible, and she just couldn't let him throw in the towel now. If Cristo really thought expanding his business was a way to somehow reconnect with his father, he had to keep trying. Somehow, someway this would all work out. "Promise me you won't give up hope."

He glanced up at her. Skepticism shone in his eyes. "You think it's still possible to strike a deal with Mr. Stravos?"

"I do."

His eyes warmed. "What would I do without you?"

"Lucky for you, you don't have to find out." She squeezed his hand. He squeezed her hand in return. When she went to pull away, he tightened his hold on her. Their fingers intertwined and they started along the beach. "I wonder why Mr. Stravos got quiet when I started talking about my family. Do you think it's possible he might know some of them?"

"I wouldn't get your hopes up. If he had known any of them, I don't see why he wouldn't have mentioned it. I'd just write off his peculiar behavior to a man who is very eccentric."

When Cristo led her straight past the walkway leading back to the lobby of the resort, she got the distinct impression his mind was too preoccupied for sleep. To be honest, she wasn't tired, either. When they reached the sand, they both slipped off their shoes. The evening air was calm and the moon was full. It was as though it had a magical pull over them.

With each step they took, her curiosity mounted about Cristo's motivation to close this deal. Maybe if she understood exactly what was at stake, she'd be better able to help him. "Why is this business deal so important to you?"

"I already explained it to you."

Kyra shook her head, knowing that his passionate need to complete this deal came from a deep personal need. "But there's something more to it. After all, the Stravos chain isn't the only hotel chain in the world. So why does it have to be this one—and why now?"

"It's not worth talking about."

"It is or I wouldn't have asked. Talk to me. I know this has something to do with your father. Do you really think your whole relationship hinges on your success?"

He stopped and turned to her. "Does that always work?"

"Does what work?"

"Wearing a man down with that sultry voice and then asking him to confide his tightly held secrets." He smiled at her letting her know that he was just teasing her.

"I guess that means it's working."

"Perhaps." He leaned forward and pressed a quick kiss to her lips.

And then as though it hadn't happened, he started walking again. Kyra didn't say anything else as she waited to learn more about the man who was holding her hand and making her heart race. She was overcome with the desire to know everything about him—at least everything that he was willing to share with her.

Just when she'd given up on him answering her, he spoke. "I was only fifteen at the time…it was Christmas break from school. We were on holiday at the family cabin in Aspen. My parents, grandparents and my three brothers were there."

So far it sounded like a lovely memory. She tried

picturing Cristo as a teenager. Something told her that he'd had a whole host of girls with crushes on him.

Cristo cleared his throat. "I didn't want to sit around the cabin and I didn't want to go into town and see the latest action movie with my older brothers. So I talked my younger brother, Max, into going skiing with me." Cristo's thumb rubbed repeatedly over the back of her hand. "It is one of those moments in life where I really wish I could go back in time and redo it. If only…"

Kyra had a sinking feeling in her stomach. She wanted to tell him to stop the story—as though that would keep the tragedy from happening. But something told her he'd kept this bottled up far too long. If he was strong enough to let out the ghosts of the past, she was strong enough to be there for him.

"Max was a really good kid and, being the youngest, he was usually left out of a lot of things my older brothers liked to do. So when I suggested we go skiing, just the two of us, he was excited. Perhaps too excited." There was a catch in Cristo's voice. He stopped walking and turned to stare out at the water. "I should have kept a better eye on him. Maybe then…"

"You were only a kid yourself. I'm sure you did your best."

"But that's just it. My best wasn't good enough." His body tensed and his grip on her hand tightened to the point of it being uncomfortable. And then, as though realizing he was causing her pain, he loosened his hold, but he didn't let go—they were still connected. "Max was showing off. He always felt a need to prove himself. Our father has always been a tough man to impress. Max must have gotten it into his head that he had to impress me, too. He went zipping by me. I tried to catch up to him but he was too far ahead and…"

Tears stung the backs of Kyra's eyes because she knew what was coming next. It was going to be horrible and unimaginable.

"And the next thing I knew…he hit a tree." Cristo's voice was raw with pain. "I watched helplessly as his body went down into the snow. And he didn't move. I tried to help him. I'd have done anything to save him."

Kyra wrapped her arms around Cristo and held him close as the waves of pain washed over him. She had no idea that his scars ran so deep, not only his brother's death, but also his estrangement from his father.

When Cristo pulled back, he started to walk again. For a few minutes they moved quietly beneath the starry sky. She didn't know what to say—what to do. Was it possible to get past Cristo's guilt?

When Cristo spoke there was a hollow tone to his voice. "After the accident, Max lived for a little bit, but the brain damage was too severe. My…my father blamed me. He said it was my fault—that I should have been looking out for Max because I was older. And he was right. I failed."

She squeezed Cristo's hand, letting him know he wasn't alone.

"My father never forgave me. I've done everything I could to make peace with him. But nothing will ever bring back Max."

"And this deal with Stravos—is this a way to prove yourself to your father?"

"It…it's a sound business decision." His gaze didn't meet hers.

Cristo couldn't admit it, but he wanted his father's approval. Kyra was at last figuring this all out. "You're intent on proving yourself…just like Max was trying to do when he had his accident."

Cristo shrugged. "My two older brothers succeeded at everything they tried. Life always came easy to them. One runs a string of golf courses and the other has a restaurant chain."

And then another thought came to her. "Are you driving yourself this hard to prove something to your father or is it something else that has you up before the sun and working until long after sundown?"

"What are you getting at?" He rubbed the back of his neck.

"That you don't believe you're worthy of happiness—of building a life for yourself—"

"I have a life."

"Going from business meeting to business meeting isn't a life. It's an existence. But you could have so much more—"

"No!" He shook his head and blinked repeatedly. "Not anymore."

Kyra wrapped her arms around Cristo and hugged him close, hoping to absorb some of his pain. "You deserve love, too."

Kyra's heart ached for the boy who'd lost his brother and the son longing for his father's love and respect. Contrary to her original impression, this deal wasn't about power or money. It was about so much more. It was about family, and she wanted desperately to reunite Cristo with his, even if she never found her own.

After a bit, Cristo pulled away. "Don't pity me. I don't deserve it. I only told you because, after all you've done for me, you deserve to know the truth—the whole truth."

"I understand and I will continue to help you any way I can. We're in this together and that's how we're going to stay."

Then without analyzing her actions, she leaned up on her tiptoes and pressed her lips to his. He didn't move at first, as though she'd caught him totally off guard. Was it really that much of a surprise after the intimate talk they'd just shared?

As her lips moved over his, she felt as though this evening they'd taken a giant leap in their relationship—less fake and more real. She knew there was no turning back now. Cristo had snuck past her neatly laid defenses and made his way into her heart.

Her hips leaned into his. Her chest pressed to his. His hands moved around to her back—to the sensitive spot where her dress dipped low. His fingers stroked her bare skin, sending the most amazing sensations zinging through her now-heated body.

She didn't want this night to end. It just kept getting better and better. If only she could be content with taking second place to his work, maybe they'd have a chance at something lasting instead of something temporary. And just like quicksand, she kept getting in deeper and deeper.

Suddenly Cristo pulled back. His gaze didn't quite meet hers. "We can't do this. It's a mistake."

A mistake?

"I'm sorry." He turned and followed the lit path back up to the lobby of the resort.

What in the world just happened?

Had he rejected her? The thought stung her heart. How could he go from opening himself up to her one minute to pushing her away the next?

The questions plagued her, one after another. And she had no answers for any of them. And the one question that bothered her most was where did they go from here?

CHAPTER THIRTEEN

WHAT IN THE world had gotten into him?

More than a week had passed since Cristo had bared his troubled soul to Kyra. And it hadn't made things better. It'd made them worse. It'd dredged up all of the horrific memories he kept locked away in the back of his mind. And when he faced Kyra, she was quiet and reserved. It wasn't just his father. Now that Kyra knew the truth, she'd withdrawn from him, too. Not that he could blame her.

Cristo moved to the bar in the suite and refilled his mug with freshly brewed coffee. His second pot that morning. And he still didn't feel like himself.

He hadn't slept well in days. He spent his nights tossing and turning. There had been no getting comfortable. All he could think about was Kyra.

They'd gotten so much closer than he'd ever intended. Even to the point where she had him opening up about his past—something he never shared with anyone. And something he would never do again.

In the daylight hours, he continued his search for

her family. He was more invested in the quest now than ever before. He needed to know that when this arrangement was over that Kyra would be all right. Because try as he might, he still hadn't convinced her to speak to her mother.

Though it was still early, Cristo had placed a call to the private investigator. He normally received weekly reports on Monday afternoons, but he had no patience to wait until after lunch. This search for Kyra's family had hit too many dead ends. They were due for a bit of good luck—at least Kyra was due it.

The conversation was short but fruitful. Cristo clenched his hand and pumped his arm as the PI gave him their first valid lead. Cristo assured the man he would personally follow up on the findings.

Determined to see this plan enacted immediately, he grabbed his phone and called his PA. He canceled all of his meetings that day. He had something more important to do. And though his PA sputtered on about the number of important meetings he would be missing, he didn't care. For once, he was putting something—rather someone—else ahead of his own business agenda. Something his father would never do.

Kyra strolled out of her bedroom, yawning as she headed for the coffeepot.

She eyed up his khaki shorts and polo shirt. "Is it casual dress day at the office?"

"No. I'm not working today."

"Really?" Her fine brows rose. "Has there been a global disaster? Is it the end of the world?"

"Kyra, stop." He didn't realize he'd turned out more like his father than he'd ever intended. A frown tugged at his lips. "Why does there have to be something wrong for me to take the day off?

"It's just that in all the time I've known you, you've never voluntarily taken a day off. So I figure something big must have happened."

Perhaps he'd been a bit too driven where his work was concerned. "It just so happens that I have other plans today."

"Well, I hope you have a good day. I have to study for a test. I've been catching up on my studies. I need to get my certification." She walked over to the coffee table and picked up her laptop. "It's time I really concentrated on my career. After all, our deal will be over soon, and I want a plan in place so that I can move on to the next stage in my life."

"Do you mean move on from me? Or the Blue Tide?"

"Both."

The wedding was in just a few weeks—the time they'd call everything off. This domestic bliss would be over. The thought of her leaving for good, of never seeing her again, was like a forceful blow to his chest. He swallowed hard. "I noticed you've been studying a lot lately. Does it have anything to do with your fight with your mother?"

"No, it doesn't. Is there something wrong with me getting serious about my future?"

"Not at all." Though he still thought she was using it as a distraction from her family problems, today wasn't the time to dwell on such things—not when at last they had a viable lead. "Could you take today off from your studies?"

She shook her head. "I have my finals soon. I almost have my hotel management certification—my ticket to see the world."

"What if I told you I heard from the investigator and he has a lead on your family?"

Her face lit up with excitement. "Really?"

Cristo nodded. "He used the picture you provided and it led him to the small village of Orchidos."

"Orchidos? I've never heard of it. Where is it?"

"You'll see. Come on." Cristo started for the door.

"Wait. Are you serious?"

"Of course I'm serious."

She ran a hand through her hair. "But I'm not ready to go anywhere. I haven't even had my first cup of coffee yet, and I'm not dressed to go out."

"You can have it in the car." He glanced at his watch. "You've got ten minutes and then we're out of here."

Kyra disappeared to her bedroom, leaving him to pace back and forth in the living room. He checked his phone every couple of minutes for texts or voice mails until he remembered that he'd had his phone calls forwarded to his PA. Today was all about Kyra.

When she emerged from her bedroom, she stole his breath away. He smothered an appreciative whistle. He didn't want to scare her off if she knew how attractive he found her. Still, he couldn't take his eyes off her.

Kyra's long hair was piled on her head with a few loose curls softening the look. A dark teal sleeveless dress with a scalloped neckline and tiny maroon flowers made her look as if she was ready for a picnic on the beach. A brown leather belt emphasized her tiny waist. The skirt ended just above her knees, showing off her legs. On her feet were jeweled flip-flops.

"Is something wrong with what I'm wearing?"

He knew he was staring but he couldn't help himself. At last her words registered in his distracted mind. "No. You look great."

"Are you sure?" She smoothed a hand down over the skirt, straightening a nonexistent wrinkle. "I could change into something else."

"No. Don't. You're perfect." In that moment, Cristo realized his words held meaning that went well beyond her clothes. There was a special quality to her—a warmth and genuineness—that appealed to him on a level he'd never felt before.

This recognition left him feeling off-kilter, not quite sure how to act around her. It was as though something significant had changed between them and yet everything was exactly the same. How was that possible?

* * *

At long last, she was about to find out a bit of her family's past. And hopefully about the present, too. She crossed her fingers for luck.

Kyra gave Cristo a sideways glance as they walked side by side through the hotel lobby. And it was all thanks to Cristo. The glass doors automatically slid open and there sat a luxury sports car—the kind of car that cost more than most people's houses.

She went to skirt around it when Cristo asked, "Where are you going? This is your ride."

"It is?" Her gaze moved from the electric-blue super car with a gold lightning bolt etched on the back fender to Cristo's smiling face. "This is yours?"

He nodded. "Why does that surprise you?"

She knew he was wealthy enough, but she didn't think he had a fun side. She thought the only entertainment he found was in closing the next big deal. Perhaps there was hope for Cristo after all. "I just didn't imagine you were the type to enjoy a sports car."

"And what type do I seem?"

"Oh, I don't know. The suit-and-tie kind. The type who reads the *Wall Street Journal* in the back of a limo. The on-the-phone-the-whole-trip type."

"Well, I'm glad to know I can surprise you from time to time." He opened the door for her and she climbed inside, enjoying the buttery soft leather upholstery and the new car smell.

Cristo moved to the driver's seat and started the

engine, which roared to life. There was no doubt in her mind that this car had power and lots of it—quite like its owner. They set off, and her body tensed as they headed down the long drive. Any minute she expected him to punch the accelerator.

"Relax." Cristo's voice was calm and reassuring. "I promise I know what I'm doing."

"That's what I'm afraid of. That you might go flying down the road like we're on a racetrack."

"You don't have to worry. You'll always be safe with me." He glanced at her briefly before focusing back on the road.

She wanted to believe him, honestly she did, but she had the distinct feeling that just being around him put her heart in jeopardy. There was something about him—something far deeper than the size of his bank account or his impressive toys—that got to her. And she would have to be careful because she wasn't about to end up playing second fiddle to a man's work—not even when the man was Cristo Kiriakas.

When her phone chimed, she retrieved it from her purse. Her mother's name appeared on the caller ID. It wasn't the first time she'd called since Kyra had uncovered her mother's deceit and it wouldn't be the last. Didn't she understand that Kyra needed to process what she'd done?

The one person Kyra thought she could always depend on had betrayed her trust. It wasn't something that could be righted—at least not straightaway.

Cristo turned down the music. "If you need to take that, go ahead. I don't mind."

Kyra sent the call to voice mail. No way was she speaking to her mother with Cristo listening. "It's not important."

"Are you sure?"

"Yes. I'll deal with it later." Much later.

Kyra turned the music back up and amused herself with the passing scenery. It kept her from staring at Cristo. Besides, she'd promised herself when she finally made it to Greece that she'd get out and see the sights, and so far she hadn't had a chance. There was so much of this beautiful country that she wanted to explore.

The car glided over the coastal roadway. The clear blue sky let the sunshine rain down over the greenery dotted with wildflowers from purples and pinks to reds and oranges. On the driver's side was a rocky cliff that led down to the beach.

Almost an hour later, they arrived in the small Greek village of Orchidos. She soon found out that the village was aptly named. Wild orchids were scattered about the perimeter of the village. Huge blooms ranged in color from apricot to maroon with splashes of white upon the delicate petals. It was truly a spectacular sight.

Cristo pulled off to the side of the road. "Are you ready?"

She eagerly nodded. "Do you really think I have any relatives living here?"

He got out and opened her door for her. "I don't know, but we have an appointment later today with the town elder. Maybe he'll have some answers for you. But first, I thought you might want to explore the village."

"I definitely do."

They passed by the modest white houses with red tile roofs. In the center of Orchidos stood a town square with a charming café, Aphrodite's. White columns surrounded the portico. And a stone carving of what she assumed was Aphrodite stood proudly in the center surrounded by little white tables.

They took a seat and were impressed with the delicious menu. When the food was delivered to their table, it did not disappoint. Kyra found herself eating far too much after Cristo ordered almost everything on the menu, from grilled fish to skewers to a salad and a number of delightful treats in between. She was beginning to think she'd never comfortably fit in her clothes again.

Next up on the agenda was walking up and down the roads and steps that connected this almost vertical village. The buildings were all different shapes and sizes. Each was steeped in history. The people of Orchidos were warm and welcoming as they offered smiles and greetings. Kyra felt right at home.

Cristo held her hand the whole time. It was as though the awkwardness they'd experienced had at last slipped away. He told her what he knew of the history of the village. Most of which he confessed to learning on the internet. They climbed wooden steps that wrapped around the hillside. The effort was well worth it as they ended up in the most stunning lookout spot, overlooking a green valley and patches of more orchids. Kyra took a bunch of photos. She thought of sending them to her mother but quickly dismissed the idea. She wasn't ready to deal with her mother. Not yet.

At one point, Cristo checked his cell phone. She waited for him to say that something had come up and he had to cut their outing short. It wouldn't surprise her in the least. Something always came between them when they were having a good time. But this time, Cristo slipped the phone back in his pocket without saying a word. She didn't mention it, either—afraid of ruining the moment.

Minutes turned into hours and before she knew it, Cristo was leading them back to the town square for coffee. It was only then she realized that her cheeks were growing sore from smiling so much. Then again, her feet ached, too. Sandals weren't the best for long walks, but she wouldn't have missed it for the world. To think her ancestors once walked these streets, too, meant a lot to her.

"Thank you for this." She smiled at Cristo. "I've really enjoyed seeing where my grandparents might have once lived. But in all of the excitement, I forgot to ask how you found this place."

"Remember that photo of your grandparents?"

When she nodded, he continued. "It was taken in this village. The building in the background once stood in the town square, but a fire destroyed it many years ago. That's why it took the investigator so long to track it down."

"So this is where my family came from?" Kyra glanced around, taking in the village with a whole new perspective.

"We had better get going. We have an appointment that I'm sure you don't want to miss."

Cristo led her a short distance to a nondescript, white stone house with the standard red tile roof, although it had a few tiles missing. He turned to her. "I hope you find your family."

She did, too. Although she already felt as though she'd found something very special with him, she wasn't ready to name those feelings. It was still so new. And she felt so vulnerable.

CHAPTER FOURTEEN

KYRA'S HEART THUMPED with anticipation.

Please let us find the answers to my past.

The red door of the house opened and an older gentleman stepped out. His tanned, wrinkled face lit up with a smile. *"Yasas."*

Kyra turned an inquiring look to Cristo, who greeted the man in fluent Greek. When Cristo turned back to her, he gave her hand a squeeze. "Our host, Tomas Marinos, welcomes you. I'm afraid he only speaks Greek. But I can ask him any questions you might have."

"Can you ask him if he knew Otis or Althea Pappas?"

Cristo translated for her and the man immediately shook his head. Disappointment sliced through her. But she wasn't giving up. They were so close.

When Cristo guided her inside the very plain house, she whispered, "Why are we staying when he doesn't know my grandparents?"

"You asked to research your family and that's what we're doing."

"Here? Shouldn't we go to the local library and search through old birth records and deeds."

He shook his head. "Not in Orchidos. There's no library. Mr. Marinos is the village elder. He has the best records of anyone, such as they are."

"Oh. I didn't know." Heat warmed her cheeks. She hadn't meant to sound unappreciative.

"I warned you in the beginning that tracking down your family based on one old photo wasn't going to be easy." Cristo's steady gaze met hers. "But I know how determined you are to find out about your past, so I used every resource at my disposal to track Mr. Marinos down and make sure he has photos and papers that stretch back to the nineteenth century. If your grandparents ever lived in Orchidos, their names will be in here."

This was it. Her stomach quivered. She was about to find out what happened to her father's family. In her excitement, she whirled around and gave Cristo a hug. "You're amazing."

"You might not say that when you see all of the papers that need sorted. I've been warned there are a lot."

She sent him a worried glance. "I don't know much Greek and—"

"No worries. I'll be right here by your side."

She nodded. In her heart, she believed her father had a hand in guiding her here. *We made it, Dad. At last we'll find out about your family.* She blinked repeatedly, still feeling the loss of her father.

The kitchen table was lined with boxes, as well as the floor. She had no doubt there was a lot of history in those boxes. She moved to the first box and yanked off the dusty lid. Finding the records were in chronological order, they were able to narrow down their search.

Cristo cocked a dark brow at her as she worked at a fervent pace. "You weren't exaggerating when you said you wanted to find your past, were you?"

She shrugged, lifting out a handful of papers. "You probably don't understand what it's like not to know where you came from. My father and I had started tracing the family tree a couple of years before he died. We started with my mother's family. Her side was pretty easy to trace. My father's side was the opposite. We planned to fly here and do research, but he…he didn't live long enough."

"And what if this information isn't what you're expecting? What if it doesn't lead you to the family you've always dreamed of?"

"I guess I'll have to let go of that dream."

"You know that sometimes the best families aren't the ones we're born into, but the ones we make for ourselves."

Kyra paused. She never would have guessed Cristo ever stopped shuffling papers and signing contracts long enough to contemplate something so deep. "Is that what you plan to do? Make a family for yourself?"

"At first, I thought my work would be enough, but lately I've been reconsidering—"

Their gazes met and her heart picked up its pace. The more this day progressed, the harder it was becoming to remember he was her business associate and not just a really sexy guy with an amazing smile. She couldn't resist his charms or ignore how he was letting his guard down around her.

She placed the aged and sun-stained papers on the table. "If you're worried you'll turn out like your father, you don't have to. I could never imagine you being cold and hostile to your child."

Cristo shook his head. "I don't know if I could split my time between my work and my family. As you've seen, I tend to get absorbed in my work. How about you? Will you choose work or family? Or will you try to balance them both?"

"I don't know what my future holds once I get my certification. I'm going to take it one day at a time."

"You know you don't have to leave the Glamour Hotel and Casino. I could find you a position—"

"No. This is something I have to do on my own."

"If you change your mind—"

"I won't."

Heat warmed her cheeks. She couldn't believe he thought that highly of her. "Thank you. But we better get started on these papers before our host kicks us out."

She glanced around, but Mr. Marinos seemed to have disappeared.

"Don't worry. He's out on the porch. But he said he'd be more than happy to answer any questions." Cristo glanced down at the papers. "Now that we've found the boxes for the right time period, how about you look through the photos and scan the papers for any mention of Pappas. If you find something of interest, you can pass it to me and I can translate it for you."

She glanced down at the papers and realized they were all in Greek. This search was going from hard to downright difficult. But she wouldn't give up. There was a part of her that needed to know where she'd come from and to connect with any relatives that still might be lurking about. And maybe then she wouldn't feel as if there was a gaping hole in her life where her father used to be.

Hours passed as they sifted over paper after paper. Frustration churned in her stomach as a whole section of papers seemed to be missing. But how could that be?

Cristo returned from speaking to Mr. Marinos. "He doesn't know what happened to the papers."

Kyra blinked away tears of frustration as she placed the lid on the box. "So that's it. We've hit a dead end. Whatever there was of my past is gone. It died with my father."

Cristo stepped around the table. He held out his hand to her and helped her to her feet. He gazed deep into her eyes. "This isn't the end. I promise. We will find out about your past. Maybe not today.

And maybe not tomorrow. But we will uncover whatever there is to find. Do you trust me?"

She wanted to—she really did. "How am I supposed to trust you when I can't even trust my own mother?"

He reached out, running a finger along her cheek. "I'm sorry she hurt you, but I am not her. I won't let you down."

Standing here so close to him with her heart pounding in her chest, she couldn't imagine him ever hurting her. "I want to trust you."

He smiled. "I'll take that as a positive sign."

All she could think about at the moment was pressing her lips to his. He really shouldn't stand this close to her. It did the craziest things to her thought processes.

And then as though he could read her thoughts, he dipped his head and placed a kiss upon her lips. He pulled away far too quickly. "Don't give up hope. Sometimes things work out when you least expect them to."

Was he referring to learning about her family?

Or was he talking about this thing that was growing between them?

She hoped it was both.

He'd been so certain this trip would give Kyra the answers she craved.

Cristo felt horrible seeing the disappointment reflected in her eyes. It was his fault. He'd put it there. He should have followed up better before mentioning the lead to her.

The sports car glided smoothly over the motorway on the drive back to the Blue Tide. Usually sitting behind the wheel of a high-performance vehicle relaxed him—gave him a new perspective on things—but not today. The disappointment in the car was palpable even though Kyra tried her best to cover it up.

His investigator had been certain Kyra would find answers in Orchidos. It didn't make sense. Who removed those papers? And why?

It was almost as if any trace of Kyra's family had been purposely removed—erased—as though they never existed. Who would do such a thing? What were they missing?

Cristo rubbed his neck. He was making too much of this. Why would anyone want to hide the history of Kyra's family? It didn't make sense.

He chanced a glance at Kyra. Her head was tilted back against the seat's headrest, and she was staring out the window. She looked as though she was all alone in this world, but that wasn't true. She had her mother and Sofia. People who cared about her, even if it wasn't the way she wanted them to care.

And she had Cristo. He cared. Perhaps he cared more than was good for either one of them. Because he didn't know how to be there for anyone. He'd never learned that as a child.

He'd been a pawn passed between his mother

and a string of nannies and then shipped off to a string of boarding schools—when he got in trouble at one, he'd get shuffled off to another. There had been no consistency—or rather he should say that his life had been one long line of inconsistencies. He could never be what Kyra had traveled the globe in search of—family. The thought saddened him. But he wasn't sure whom he was sadder for, her or himself.

Still, he hated seeing Kyra in such turmoil. He couldn't just sit by and let her feel so dejected—so alone.

He moved his hand from the gearshift and reached out to her. But with her arms crossed, he couldn't reach her hand, so he settled for her thigh. Big miscalculation on his part. A sense of awareness took hold of his very eager body. His fingertips tingled where the heat of her body permeated the cottony material of her summer dress.

Kyra's head turned and their gazes met. He glanced back at the road, relieved to have an excuse to keep her from reading the conflicting emotions in his eyes. He knew he should pull his hand away, but he couldn't—not yet. He hadn't made his point yet.

"Kyra, you're not alone." He tightened his hold on her thigh and his pulse quickened. "You've got people who care about you."

"Does that include you?"

The breath caught in his throat. What was she

asking him? Did she mean as a friend? Or did she want something more? Right then the urge was overwhelming to pull back—to keep a safe distance. But a glance at the emotional turmoil in her eyes had him keeping their physical link for just a bit longer.

"I'm here as your friend anytime that you need me." *There. That sounded good. Didn't it?*

His cell phone buzzed. He knew he'd promised not to do any work today, but sometimes promises had to be broken. And this was one of those times when he desperately needed a diversion.

He glanced at the phone as it rested in the console. "It's Niko Stravos. I think I should get it, don't you?"

"You're asking me?" The surprise in her voice reflected his own. He'd never asked anyone if he should take a call. When the phone buzzed again, Kyra added, "Answer it. Maybe he has good news. I could use some about now."

Cristo pressed a button on the steering wheel and, utilizing the car's speaker system, said, "Hello."

"Cristo, it's Niko." They continued to make pleasantries and Cristo let him know that he was on the speakerphone and Kyra was with him. "Sounds like I have perfect timing, then. I'd like to invite you both back for dinner later this week."

Cristo, surprised by the invitation, cast Kyra a glance, finding she looked equally shocked. "Thank you. But perhaps we should get together at my resort. Your grandfather wasn't happy about our prior visit—"

"I wouldn't worry about that. My grandfather can be temperamental at times. Don't take it personally." There was a bit of static on the phone line, but soon it quieted and Niko's voice came through clearly. "In fact, this dinner invitation was my grandfather's idea. He sends his apologies for being abrupt the last time you were here and asks that you join us for a more casual dinner Friday night."

Really? What could this possibly mean? Cristo sure wanted to find out. But he knew Kyra had been disappointed by her lack of discovery today, and he didn't know if she'd be up for putting on a happy front for the senior Stravos.

They were almost back at the Blue Tide Resort now. Cristo slowed the car and turned into the long drive. Cristo hated that he might have to back out of this amazing opportunity, but Kyra's needs had to come first. "Can you hold for just a moment?"

"Sure."

"Thanks." Cristo muted the phone in order to speak with Kyra in private. "What do you think?"

She picked at a nonexistent piece of lint on her sundress. "I think it's an amazing opportunity for you. You should go and see what Nikolaos Stravos has to say."

"And what about you? Will you come with me, too?"

CHAPTER FIFTEEN

PLEASE LET HER AGREE.

After all, they were a team.

Cristo prompted her, anxious for an answer. "Kyra?"

She worried her bottom lip. "I don't know. I really wasn't much help to you on the last visit. You might be better off on your own."

He wanted to argue with her and tell her they made a great team, but he held back the words. After she'd just put him on the spot about being in her life, he didn't want to confuse things further. He was already confused enough.

"I understand." He tightened his fingers on the steering wheel. "After today's adventure, you need some time to regroup. I'll let Niko know."

"Thank you for understanding."

Cristo pressed the button for the phone. "Niko?"

"Yes. By the way, I forgot to mention that my grandfather requested Kyra bring any photos she might have of her family. He said he might have some information for her."

Kyra's face lit up with anticipation—it was such a welcome sight. Cristo didn't have to ask if she'd had a change of heart. He just hoped Nikolaos Stravos's information was better than what they'd uncovered today, which was nothing. "We'll be there."

Niko gave them the details, including the request for casual dress. Cristo knew that the Stravoses' version of casual dress was far from jeans and T-shirts. It was more like a suit minus the tie. Which satisfied Cristo just fine. He always felt more in his element when he was dressed up.

He pulled the car into his reserved spot. One of the attendants would clean it before putting it in his private garage. Right now, the care of his prized car slid to the back of his mind. He turned in his seat. "You did it. Thank you."

Her fine brows drew together. "I did what?"

"Got us a second chance to impress Nikolaos Stravos—"

"I just wish it was under different circumstances. I don't like the tales we're fabricating." Anxiety reflected in her eyes. "What if I say the wrong thing? What if he figures out the truth?"

Cristo didn't like this situation any better than her. This wasn't the way he normally did business, but how else were you supposed to negotiate with someone who was so stubborn and set in their ways?

But this relationship wasn't all a lie. No matter how much he fought it, there was definitely something growing between him and Kyra. He couldn't put a name on it. He just knew that she deserved better than him.

"You'll do fine. You'll charm him just like you do everyone." Anxious to erase the worry from her big, beautiful eyes, Cristo leaned over in his seat and pressed his lips to hers.

She didn't move at first. Had he caught her off guard? His muscles tensed, preparing to be rejected.

And then her mouth started to move beneath his. He started to relax—to enjoy the touch. She tasted sweet like vine-ripened grapes. He doubted he'd ever have another sip of wine without thinking of her.

Cristo had only meant to give her a reassuring kiss, but now that his lips were touching hers, he had no interest in pulling away. What he wanted was more of this—more of Kyra. And she didn't seem to be complaining as her fingers lifted to caress his jaw. No other woman could turn him on the way Kyra could. It wasn't even as if she tried. It was just natural—chemistry.

As her fingertips trailed down his neck to the inside of his shirt collar, he knew he had to stop her before things got totally out of hand. This was not the place to take things to the next level. His fingers moved to cover hers, halting their exploration.

With every bit of willpower, he pulled back and stared her in the eyes. "Now, was that a lie?"

She shook her head. "But—"

His lips pressed to hers again, silencing her protest. He didn't want to know what followed her *but*, not at all. They'd tackled enough problems for now.

He rested his forehead against hers. "No buts. There's something between us. Don't ask me to define it because I can't. And don't expect too much from me because I don't want to let you down. The only thing I can offer you is this—right here, right now."

She pulled away from him. "All the more reason for me not to go to this dinner with you."

"And miss out on a chance to find out what Nikolaos might know about your family?" He knew he had her there. Finding out about her past was too important to her to back out now. "Don't worry, I'll be right there next to you the whole time." He'd just reached for the door handle when Kyra spoke up.

"Do you really think keeping up this charade is the right way to go about things with Stravos? Maybe if we explain everything to him, he'll understand the importance of the deal."

There was nothing about Nikolaos Stravos in his past or present that in the slightest way hinted he was an understanding man who could be swayed by sentimentality. He had a cutthroat reputation in the business world—he wasn't used to sitting back and letting people have their way.

But Kyra had a point. Cristo wasn't comfortable with weaving such an elaborate ruse. "Why don't we play it by ear?"

She stared at him for a moment before nodding her head. "If you think it's best."

As they exited the car and headed back to their suite, Cristo couldn't dismiss her words. He didn't want Kyra thinking less of him. He wasn't conducting this elaborate ruse because it was fun, although it was with Kyra, or because it was his normal business practice, which it certainly wasn't, but rather because it was what this particular situation necessitated.

His father had taught him to do anything necessary to secure an important business deal. After all, business came first, ahead of all else including family. Cristo supposed he'd learned that lesson quite well. Maybe too well. That was why he'd chosen not to have a family. He didn't want to end up like his father.

And in that moment, he recalled something he'd promised himself as a teenager. After observing his father at the office and witnessing the unhappiness he unleashed on a regular basis, Cristo swore he'd do things differently. Less skirting the truth and with more compassion.

So far he was failing.

Perhaps it was time he considered doing things Kyra's way.

Sleep was elusive.

Kyra tiptoed through the darkened suite late Thursday night. Cristo needed his rest. He had a big day tomorrow. And hopefully Nikolaos Stravos had changed his mind and had decided to go ahead with the sale.

But more than that, she wondered what the older man wanted with her. She recalled their prior meeting and the way the man had stared at her before storming off. He didn't like her, so why was he suddenly willing to help her? Something wasn't adding up, but she couldn't put her finger on exactly what it was.

She sighed and leaned against the wall surrounding the balcony that overlooked the private cove. She was letting her imagination get the best of her. It was Cristo's fault. Ever since their outing, she hadn't been able to get him off her mind. She'd finally found out what it was like to have all of his attention and now she craved more.

"Would you mind some company?"

The sound of Cristo's voice caused her to jump. She turned and had to struggle to keep from gaping at his bare chest and the low-slung dark boxers. Had she fallen asleep somewhere along the way and this was a dream—a very vivid, very tempting dream?

She swallowed hard. "Did I wake you?"

He raked his fingers through his already mussed-up hair. "That would imply I was actually sleeping."

"You couldn't sleep, either?"

"No." He moved to stand next to her. "It's a beautiful night. The moon is so full that it's almost like daylight. But I have a feeling that's not why you're out here. What's bothering you?"

She didn't want to get into another conversation

about Nikolaos Stravos. Instead, she said, "I couldn't sleep, and I was bored of staring into the dark."

He reached out and put a finger beneath her chin, pulling her around to face him. "Are you still worried about the dinner?"

"It's nothing."

"I don't believe you. Your eyes tell a different story."

"They do?" She glanced away. Did they say how sexy she found him right now? Did he know how hard it was for her to carry on this conversation when he was barely dressed?

"Obviously you have something on your mind, and until you deal with it, you'll be left lurking in the shadows of the night." His voice lowered, making it warm and quite inviting. "Talk to me."

What would he say if she told him what was weighing on her mind at this particular moment? Her gaze once again dipped to his bare chest. His presence was distracting her—teasing her—tempting her.

How did someone look that good? Cristo certainly knew his way around a weight room. How did a busy man like him have time for exercise? Somehow he fit it in between boardroom meetings and jet-setting around the globe.

"Kyra? What is it?"

She struggled to center her thoughts on something besides how her heart was thump-thumping in her chest. She licked her dry lips. "I…I was just wondering if this is all going to end tomorrow. You know, after the meeting with Stravos. Will you and I go our separate ways?"

"Is that what you want?"

Her gaze met his. She really didn't want this thing between them to end. She was getting totally caught up in this world of make-believe. And what would it hurt for it to go on just a little longer?

Cristo reached out to her, running the back of his fingers down her cheek. "Tell me what you want."

The pounding of her heart echoed in her ears. Her mouth opened but nothing came out. Her mind went blank. Sometimes words just weren't enough. Without giving thought to the consequences, she lifted up on her tiptoes and leaned forward. Her lips pressed to his.

This was most definitely what she wanted.

His hands gripped her hips, pulling her closer. Her breasts pressed against his muscled chest. Her palms landed on the smooth skin of his shoulders. It was as though an electrical pulse zinged through her fingertips and raced through her body. Every part of her body was alert and needy.

Their kiss moved from tentative to heated in less time than it took his fancy sports car to reach cruising speed. And her engine was revved up and ready to go. Tonight she wasn't going to think about the future or the implications of where this most enticing night would leave them. This moment was all about letting down their guards and savoring the time they had together.

Cristo pulled back. His breath was deep and fast. His heated gaze met hers. "Kyra, are you sure about this?"

She nodded. She'd never been so sure about anything in her life. That not-so-long-ago night when he'd proposed to her, he'd utterly charmed her. But today when they'd toured Orchidos, he'd finally cracked the wall around her heart.

If she walked away now, she would regret it for the rest of her life. Her time with Cristo was the stuff that amazing memories were made of. And she wanted a piece of him to take with her—a tender, special moment.

"I'm sure." Her voice came out as a whisper in the breeze. "I've never been more certain."

His lips claimed hers again. His kiss was hungry and rushed, like a drowning man seeking oxygen. Her hands wrapped around his neck. The curves of her body pressed to the solid muscles of his toned body.

In that moment, she could no longer hide from the truth. She loved Cristo. He hadn't snuck around, no, he'd marched right past her defenses and staked a claim to her heart. She'd tried ignoring it and then denying it, but the truth was she loved him.

As though he sensed her surrender, he stopped kissing her long enough to sweep her off her feet. Her pulse raced. If she was dreaming, she never wanted to wake up.

This night would be unforgettable.

CHAPTER SIXTEEN

THE GLARE OF sunshine had a way of making things look different than they had in the shadows of the night.

Kyra had absolutely no idea what to say to Cristo. So she'd avoided him all day, hoping the words would eventually come to her. But by evening, she was even more confused by her emotions.

Where exactly had their night of lovemaking left them? After all, it wouldn't have happened if not for their make-believe relationship. This whole web of role-playing and innuendos was confusing everything. And now they'd just succeeded in compounding matters even further.

As she recalled the magical night of whispered sweet nothings and the flurry of kisses, her heart fluttered. But was this rush of emotions real? Or was it a side effect of their fake romance? How was she to know?

The only abundantly clear fact was that she would have to be extremely careful going forward. Otherwise, her heart would end up smashed to smithereens when this elaborate ruse was over. And she had no doubt this relationship would most definitely end, sooner rather than later. Cristo had made that crystal clear.

Kyra stepped up to the floor-length mirror in her bedroom and examined her little black dress. It certainly wasn't anything fancy by any stretch, but she wasn't sure what casual dress entailed. So in her mind, a little black dress seemed to work for all occasions—she hoped.

There was a tap on her bedroom door followed by Cristo's voice. "Kyra, are you ready?"

"Um, yes. I'll be right there." There was no time for second-guessing or trying on yet another dress. She was going with black. She snatched up a small black purse with delicate beading on the front and headed for the door, hoping this evening would go much better than their first encounter with Mr. Stravos.

On not-so-steady legs, she made her way to the living room, where Cristo was waiting for her. He looked breathtakingly handsome in a stylish navy suit with a light blue shirt. The top buttons were undone and conjured up memories—heated, needy memories. How in the world was she supposed to get through the evening when she was so utterly distracted?

Cristo gave her outfit a quick once-over. "You look beautiful. Are you ready to go?"

She nodded, still uncertain where things stood between them and not sure how to broach the subject.

Apparently she wasn't the only one unsure, because she noticed how Cristo was careful to avoid the subject, too. In fact, he was quieter than normal. It only succeeded in increasing her nervousness.

Once again, they were whisked away in the helicopter. This time she welcomed the *whoop-whoop* of the rotary blades. It was a perfectly legitimate excuse to remain quiet. The only problem was the ride was much too short, and before she was ready, they touched down at the Stravos estate.

This time Niko came out to greet them. "I must apologize for my grandfather. He is delayed by an overseas phone call. But have no worries, he will be joining us."

Cristo gave each sleeve of his suit a tug. "Do you know why he wanted to meet with us?"

Kyra translated that to mean *Is he interested in making a deal?* She had to admit she was quite curious, too. Because she had a distinct feeling her future with Cristo hinged on what happened this evening. And she wasn't ready to let him go, not yet. They'd finally turned a corner in their relationship and she was anxious to see if there was anything real—anything lasting.

Tonight, dinner was served outside in the courtyard. Lanterns were lit and strategically placed around the area, providing a cozy ambience.

"Kyra?" It was Cristo's voice and it held a note of concern.

She glanced over to find both men staring at her.

"Um, sorry. I was just trying to memorize the layout of this patio area. I'd love to have something similar someday."

Cristo arched a brow, but he didn't ask any questions. "Niko asked if you'd care for something to drink."

"Yes, please. Would you happen to have any iced tea?"

Niko smiled and nodded. "I'll get that for you."

She was surprised to see her host move to the cart of refreshments and pour her a glass of tea. For some reason, she imagined there would be servants tripping over themselves to do Niko's bidding. Apparently this billionaire was quite self-sufficient. Maybe that was why she liked him so much. And she noticed Cristo had warmed up to him, too.

Kyra struck up a conversation about the architecture of Niko's home and its rich history. Cristo surprised her with his knowledge of Greek history. Little by little, she found herself relaxing.

"Excuse me." A voice came from across the courtyard. Conversation immediately ceased as all heads turned to find Mr. Stravos making his way toward them. "Apologies. Work waits for no man."

Cristo got to his feet. Kyra followed his lead, anxious for this visit to go better than the last one. She lifted her lips into what she hoped was a warm smile even though her insides shivered with anxiety. She noticed that Mr. Stravos didn't smile. Was he angry? Or was that his usual demeanor?

After shaking hands with Cristo, the older man turned to her. He took her hand in his, and instead of shaking it, he lifted it to his lips and pressed a feathery kiss to the back of her hand. She continued to hold her smile in place.

Well, he definitely isn't angry. What a relief.

"Thank you for coming back to visit, my dear. I'm sorry our previous time together was so brief."

"Thank you for the invitation. I was just telling Niko how lovely I find your courtyard. Someday I'd love to have a similar one." She struggled to make polite chatter when all she wanted to do was question the man about her family.

Mr. Stravos glanced around as though he'd forgotten what it looked like. "I must admit that I don't spend much time out here these days. Most of my time is spent in my office."

"You must be quite busy. Too bad it takes you away from this gorgeous courtyard and the amazing flower gardens surrounding your home."

As though on cue, dinner was served at the glass table on the other side of the courtyard. The conversation turned to their adventure to Orchidos. Cristo joined in, explaining that it was also his first visit to the village. Everyone took a turn talking about subjects from the wild orchids growing throughout the village to the architecture.

After dinner, everyone moved to the cushioned chairs grouped together. Cristo took her hand and gave it a squeeze. Her gaze moved to meet his. He smiled at her and her heart tumbled in her chest. No man had ever made her feel so special.

"How long are you going to continue with this charade?" Mr. Stravos asked out of the blue.

Kyra's gaze swiftly moved to the older man. His expression was perfectly serious. They'd been busted. And try as she might, she couldn't keep the heat of embarrassment from rushing to her cheeks.

Cristo's neck muscles flexed as he swallowed. "What charade?"

"This." The man waved his hand between him and Kyra. "You think I'm going to sell you my hotels because you put on a show of marrying her. You two hardly know each other. Am I really supposed to believe that you care for her?"

Kyra hoped Cristo knew what to say because her mind was a blank. If she tried to speak now, it'd be nothing more than stuttering and floundering.

"You're right." Cristo released her hand and sat forward. "I knew how important marriage is to you and I wanted you to take my proposal seriously, so I asked Kyra to act as my fiancée." When the older man's gaze moved her way, Cristo added, "Don't be upset with her. She didn't want to do it, but I convinced her. And a lot has changed since then."

Kyra was not about to let Cristo shoulder all of the blame. The more she got to know Cristo, the more she realized how important this deal was to him. "He has been nothing but kind and generous. I couldn't ask for anyone better in my life." Her gaze moved to the man who'd rocked her world the night before. His gaze met hers. In that moment, she had her answer—their lovemaking hadn't been faked. There was something genuine between them.

Mr. Stravos scoffed at her defense of Cristo. "He is only looking out for himself. He wants this deal so much that he will do anything to get it."

"That's not true. He's been helping me track down my family. It's what led us to Orchidos." She sighed, still disappointed they hadn't unearthed any new information. "But we weren't able to come up with any further information. Which is strange because the investigator traced the photo I have back to that village."

The older man's dark eyes narrowed. "Do you have the photo with you?"

At last she'd gained his attention and hopefully his help. "I do." She reached into her purse and withdrew the black-and-white photo. She held it out to the man. "That's my grandmother and grandfather. They both died before I was born."

The man didn't say a word as he retrieved his reading glasses from his jacket pocket. He moved the photo closer to the lantern to get a better look. Did he recognize someone? The longer he stared at the photo, the more hope swelled in her chest. What did he know about her family? Would he be able to point her in the right direction?

She sat up straight and laced her fingers together to keep from fidgeting. As though sensing her mounting anxiousness, Cristo reached out to her. His fingers wrapped gently around her forearm and gave her a squeeze before sliding down to her hand. She unclenched her fingers in order to hold his hand.

Her gaze met his, where she found comfort and reassurance. It helped calm her racing heart. No matter what Mr. Stravos said, she knew instinctively that Cristo would be there to help her deal with the news.

Mr. Stravos tapped the photo with his finger. "You're sure this is your family?"

Kyra nodded. The breath hitched in her throat. She had the feeling her life was about to take a drastic turn. She just hoped it was for the best.

There was a long pause before Mr. Stravos spoke again. "I…I knew your grandmother."

Really? There was sincerity written all over his aging face. She expelled the pent-up breath, but she was still cautious. "Why didn't you say so when I told you her name?"

"Because I had to be sure it was her. You don't understand."

"You're right. I don't understand at all. Why would you keep it a secret that you knew her?"

"Because she's my sister. And you aren't the first person to come here claiming to be my long-lost relative—"

"I never claimed to be anything of the sort." She

could feel Cristo's grip on her tightening just a bit—cautioning her to move carefully.

"I am sorry." The man's voice was barely more than a whisper. "I've grown too cautious over the years."

She had the feeling the apology was rare for him. His words touched her and immediately soothed her lingering ire. "Trust me. I didn't come here expecting or wanting anything from you. We…we should go."

"No. Stay. Please. We have much to talk about."

She cast Cristo a hesitant look. He nodded his consent. She settled back in her seat and coffee was poured. She tried to relax but she was too wound up, waiting and wondering what information Mr. Stravos would have about her grandparents.

"I haven't seen my sister since I was a kid. She was older than me. Many years ago, our family lived in Orchidos."

"I don't understand. Cristo and I just spent a day there, talking with people and searching through old papers. There was no hint of your family or my grandmother."

Her uncle nodded in understanding. "That's because I had some problems in the past with blackmail. I had as much of my family's history that could be located gathered and brought to me. And the people of Orchidos who knew my family promised to keep what they knew to themselves. Having money comes with challenges that some might not expect. Privacy comes at a premium."

"And how do you know I'm not lying to you?" She didn't like being even remotely lumped in with blackmailers and scam artists.

"That's easy, my dear. You look like my sister when she was younger. When I first saw you, I thought I'd seen a ghost."

Which explained why he'd made such a hasty exit after their first meeting. "But I don't understand. Why don't you know what happened to my grandmother? Did you two have a falling-out?"

"No. We didn't. But she had one with our father. She'd fallen in love with a boy my father didn't approve of. My father did everything possible to break them up but nothing worked. When they eloped, my father disowned her and told her she was never welcome in his home again."

A deep sadness came over Kyra. She couldn't imagine what it would be like for her grandmother to have to choose between the man she loved and her family. "That must have been horrible for all of you."

"There was no reasoning with my father. He was a big man who ruled the household with an iron fist. And he never backed down from a decision."

"So my grandmother married my grandfather and moved to the States?"

Her uncle nodded. "That night was the last time I saw her. My mother and I were banned from keeping in contact with her. When I got older, I thought about checking on her, but back in those days there was no such thing as the internet—no easy way to find someone who didn't want to be found."

They continued to talk and fit together the puzzle pieces of her grandmother's life. And then the conversation turned to Kyra and her life. Uncle Nikolaos seemed genuinely interested in her. He at last let down his guarded exterior, showing her a warm and approachable side.

When she glanced around, she found Cristo and Niko deep in conversation. This evening had turned out quite differently than she'd imagined. And it was all thanks to Cristo. If it wasn't for him, she never would have met her uncle and cousin.

As though Cristo could sense she was thinking about him, he glanced over at her and smiled. Just that small gesture sent a warm, fuzzy feeling zinging through her chest. She loved him more than she'd ever loved anyone. And she knew it was dangerous, because in the end, she would get hurt. But for this evening, she was going to bask in the warmth she found being in the company of the man she loved and her newfound family.

Cristo had a hard time taking his eyes off Kyra.

There was something different about her that night. Was it that dress? Or was she glowing with happiness from finding her long-lost family? Whatever it was, she was even more captivating than before, if that was possible.

"My cousin seems to be charming my grandfather. That's not an easy feat. Trust me. I've tried in the past. That man is quite set in his ways."

"They do seem to be hitting it off." Cristo finished his coffee. He was tired of dancing around the subject. "What do you think my chances are of putting together a deal to buy the hotel chain?"

"Honestly, I've talked with my grandfather at some length and so far he hasn't shown any interest in parting with it. Between you and me, I think it goes far deeper than a business deal. But for the life of me, I can't figure out why he holds so tightly to it, and he won't explain it to me."

Cristo could feel his chance to seal this deal slipping away. And he'd run out of ideas of how to get through to Nikolaos Stravos, who took stubborn to a whole new level.

Niko set his empty coffee cup on a small table before turning back to Cristo. "I think your best hope lies with your fiancée." His brows drew together. "She's still your fiancée, isn't she?"

Without hesitation, Cristo nodded. "She is. If she'll still have me." A thought came to Cristo of a way to make Kyra happy. "Since you're now family, how would you feel about standing up for me at the wedding?"

Niko's eyes opened wide. "I'd be honored."

"Great." The men shook hands. "Kyra will be so happy."

Cristo turned to gaze over at his adorable fiancée. He didn't know how it had happened, but somewhere along the way, he'd begun to picture her in his future. In fact, he couldn't imagine life without her in it. Marriage would undoubtedly change things as he knew them, but he instinctively knew it would be better with her in it.

When it was time to call it a night, hugs were exchanged between Kyra and her newfound family. Cristo couldn't be happier for her and it had nothing to do with his business…or his hopes to iron out a deal with Stravos.

Nikolaos gave him a stern look. "No more charades. Honesty is the only sound basis for a relationship. And my great-niece deserves only the best."

"I'll do my best, sir."

Nikolaos arched a brow. "You should also know that your involvement with my niece will have no bearing on my decision about selling the hotel chain. Do not have her doing your bidding."

Cristo's body stiffened. "The thought never crossed my mind."

The man's cold, hard gaze left no doubt about his sincerity. "Good. Because if you do, mark my words, I will use every resource at my disposal to destroy you."

Cristo bristled at the threat, but he willed himself not to react for Kyra's sake. At long last, she'd found the family she had been longing for—a connection to the father she lost—and Cristo refused to be the reason for discord between them.

Noting the obvious affection in the older man's eyes when they strayed to Kyra, Cristo understood the man's protectiveness. Cristo cleared his throat. "I would expect nothing less of a caring uncle. I am glad you have found each other."

Nikolaos's eyes momentarily widened as though surprised by Cristo's response. "So long as we understand each other."

"We do, sir. We both want Kyra to be happy." And he truly meant it.

Approval reflected in Nikolaos's eyes. "If you two decide to go through with the wedding, I'd very much like to be there."

"You would?" Kyra interjected. A smile lit up her face.

"Most definitely."

Cristo held out his hand to the man. "We'll definitely keep in touch."

Nikolaos cleared his throat. "As for your offer to buy the hotel chain, I will take it under advisement. My grandson seems to think it would be a good idea to divest ourselves of it and focus on our shipping sector, but I like to remain diversified." He glanced down at Cristo's extended hand, then accepted it with a firm grip and solid shake. "I will take your offer to our advisers and see what they have to say."

"Thank you. I appreciate your consideration."

Cristo didn't know what would happen with his business deal, but he was starting to figure out that the most important thing right now was his future with Kyra.

CHAPTER SEVENTEEN

"I CAN'T BELIEVE IT," Kyra spoke into the phone the next morning.

The sound of footsteps on the tiled floor had her glancing over her shoulder. The sight of Cristo made her heart go *tip-tap-tap.* She smiled at him and he returned the gesture. There was just something about his presence that made her stomach quiver with excitement. He headed straight for the coffeemaker.

"Sofia, I've got to go. I'll talk to you later."

Kyra rushed off the phone. She couldn't stop smiling. She told herself it was because she'd connected with her father's family. And though it wasn't exactly the family she'd been expecting, it was a connection to her father nonetheless. That connection was priceless, especially in light of the discord between her and her mother.

"You can't believe what?"

"I'm just so surprised we found my family. Honestly, after we ran into nothing but dead ends in Orchidos, I'd pretty much given up hope of finding anyone or learning anything about my father's family. I can't believe I've found them."

"I'm really happy for you."

Maybe this was the opening she needed to help Cristo find his way back to his family, which was so much more important than the business deal—if only he could see that.

"Do you really mean that?"

"Of course I do. I know how important family is to you."

"It's just as important to you." When he shook his head, she persisted. "It is, or you wouldn't be so tormented by the memory of your brother or doing everything in your power to gain your father's respect."

He continued to shake his head. "You don't know what you're saying."

"This wedding, it could be a bridge back to them." She had no idea if he was listening to anything she was saying, but she couldn't give up. Someone had to make him see reason.

His dark brows drew together as his disbelieving gaze met hers. "And how is that going to work? Invite them here for a doomed wedding? I'm sure that'll really impress them."

"You're missing the point. This isn't about impressing anyone—it's about reconnecting, talking, spending time together. They'll understand when the wedding is canceled for legitimate reasons."

He raked his fingers through his hair. “Why is this so important to you?”

“Because it’s important to you. Just promise me that you’ll think about it.”

He hesitated. “I’ll think about it. By the way, you’re welcome to visit with your uncle and cousin as much as you want. Just let me know ahead of time and I’ll have the helicopter available. I know you’re really missing your mother—”

A frown pulled at Kyra’s face. “I don’t want to talk about her.”

“Wait a second. You’re allowed to lecture me on making amends with my family and yet you’re unwilling to deal with your own mother?”

“It’s different.”

“Uh-huh.” His tone held a distinct note of disbelief. “And how would that be?”

Kyra huffed. “Because she lied and manipulated me.”

“One of these days you’re going to have to take her call.”

“Not today.” Kyra glanced at the clock, finding it was already after eight o’clock. She turned back to Cristo. “Speaking of family, I’ve received RSVPs from your brothers. They send their regrets.”

“I told you they’d be too busy to travel halfway around the world for a wedding.” His tone was matter-of-fact. “That’s why I asked Niko to stand up for me.”

“You did?” This was news to her.

Cristo nodded. "And he agreed. So no worries about my absentee brothers."

The fact he hadn't expected more from his brothers was disheartening. She didn't like the distance between Cristo and his family. Maybe it was because the only family she had now was her mother, but Kyra didn't think there was anything more important than staying in contact with those you cared about.

"I just can't believe they'd miss their brother's wedding."

"Believe it. The apple doesn't fall far from the tree."

"What does that mean?"

"It means they are a lot like my father. Business first. Family a distant second."

How sad.

"Were you ever close?"

"My brothers are a lot older than me. Eight and ten years. It wasn't like we had much in common. I was much closer to Max."

And when Max died, Cristo was left alone with his guilt. *How awful.* She wanted to help him find a way back to his family.

"Maybe if you were to call your brothers—maybe if they knew how important this is to you—"

"No." His voice held a note of finality. "I'm fine on my own."

"Are you? Or are you punishing yourself for Max's accident—something that wasn't your fault?"

"You don't know what you're talking about."

"Don't I?"

She wasn't going to back down and let him waste the rest of his life in a mire of guilt for something that wasn't his fault. "You keep thinking that if you'd said something different or done something different that the accident could have been averted, don't you? It's easier to blame yourself than to accept it was totally out of your hands." Her voice wobbled. "Nothing would have changed what happened."

Cristo's brows scrunched together. "You sound like you're talking from experience."

"I am." She'd never told anyone this. "For a long time, I blamed myself for my father's death."

"But why? I thought he died of a heart attack."

"He did. At home. Alone. My mother had driven me to the movies to meet one of my friends. My mother went shopping until it was time to pick me up. There wasn't anyone there to help him. To call 911."

Cristo moved to her side and wrapped an arm around her shoulders, pulling her close. She let her weight lean into him. Together they could prop each other up. "It wasn't your fault."

"Just like it wasn't your fault."

Cristo didn't say anything, which she took as a good sign. Hopefully he'd let go of the guilt that was only succeeding in distancing him from his family.

Kyra blinked repeatedly, trying to stuff her emotions down deep inside. "Shouldn't you be at a meeting or something?"

His brows lifted. "Are you trying to get rid of me?"

"Not at all. It's just that you're always so busy."

He took a sip of coffee before returning the cup to the bar. "You're right. I am a busy man. Maybe too busy."

"Too busy? Where did that come from?"

"I've been thinking about what you said about slowing down."

Really? He'd listened to something she'd said to him. He certainly had her attention now. "And what did you decide?"

"That there's more to life than work."

It was a good thing she had her hip against the couch or she might have fallen over. Since when did this workaholic have time for fun? "What have you done with the real Cristo?"

"I'm serious."

So it appeared. But she did have to wonder how far he was willing to take this makeover. "And what do you have in mind?"

"I saw there's a beach volleyball game this morning. I signed us up."

Her mouth gaped. She had to admit that she never expected those words to come out of his mouth. Not in a million years.

"You do play volleyball, don't you? I thought I overheard you mention it to Sofia."

She nodded. "I played all through high school. It wasn't beach volleyball, but it'll do."

"Good. How soon can you be ready?" There

was a knock at the door. "That will be breakfast. I thought you'd want something to eat first."

"Are there any other surprises I should be aware of?"

He sent her a lopsided grin. "I don't know. Would you like some more?"

This playful side of Cristo was new to her, but she fully approved. A smile pulled at her lips as her gaze met his. She wanted the day to slow down so they could enjoy this time together a bit longer. Okay, a lot longer.

He held up a finger for her to wait as he went to answer the door. After the wide array of food had been delivered and arranged on the table, he turned back to her. "Now, what were we discussing? Oh, yes, surprises. Do you want more of them?"

She didn't have to contemplate the answer. "Yes, more surprises as long as they are this good." She lifted one of the silver lids from a plate, finding scrambled eggs, sausage, bacon and orange wedges. She grabbed a slice of orange and savored its citrusy taste. Once she'd finished it and set aside the rind, she turned back to him. "Definitely."

He moved to stand in front of her, and before she knew what he was up to, his head dipped. His lips claimed hers. His mouth moved tentatively over hers. Was he testing the waters? The thought that he wasn't as sure of himself as he liked the world to think turned her on all the more.

She met him kiss for kiss, letting him know that

his advance was quite welcome. Her arms wound their way around his neck as his hands spanned her waist, pulling her snug against him. She definitely liked his surprises.

Much too soon, he pulled back. "Don't pout."

It showed? Or was he just getting to know her that well? "But I liked that surprise. A lot."

He smiled broadly. She loved how his eyes twinkled with merriment. It filled her with a happiness she'd never known before. She forced her lips into a playful frown, hoping to get more of his steamy kisses.

He shook his head. "It isn't going to work. You'll have to wait until later."

"You promise?"

"I do. But right now, we have some beach volleyball to get to."

"You're really serious about this, aren't you?" For some reason, she never pictured Cristo as the volleyball type. But then again, with his shirt off and some board shorts hung low on his trim waist...she could envision it clearly now.

"Yes, I'm serious. And if you don't go change quickly, we won't have time to eat."

Kyra groaned as he pushed her in the direction of her bedroom to put on her bikini. This day was definitely going to be interesting. Very interesting indeed.

How could more than two weeks have flown by?

Cristo had never had so much fun.

He'd really enjoyed this time with Kyra. There had been the volleyball tournament followed by leisurely strolls along the beach. There were late mornings wrapped in each other's arms followed by early evenings for more of the same. If only he'd known what he'd been missing all of this time, he might have taken the chance on love sooner.

Somewhere between the moonlit walks on the beach, the stories of her childhood and the stroll through a nearby village, he'd fallen for his own pretend bride. Now he wanted her for his very genuine wife. But how could he prove his honest intentions to her without her thinking he had an ulterior motive?

His feelings for her were not fleeting. This was not a summer romance to reflect upon in his twilight years. No, this was a deep down, can't-live-without-her love. But he knew Kyra was still holding back—clinging to that wall around her heart.

And he knew why—the fake engagement they'd struck at the beginning followed by her mother's betrayal. Combine them both and it was no wonder Kyra was having problems trusting him. But there had to be a way to convince her of his sincerity. But how?

While Kyra was off checking on flowers for the wedding, he found himself pacing back and forth in the suite. She had left him with one task to complete for the wedding—one task that left his gut knotted up. He had to make a phone call to his parents.

He withdrew his phone from his pocket. His finger hovered over the screen. He'd been very selective on which calls to take this week and which to let pass to his voice mail. Did that make him irresponsible? His father would say it did, but Cristo was beginning to see things quite differently. Every person deserved some downtime now and then. Everyone deserved time to find happiness and love.

And he wouldn't have realized any of this if it wasn't for Kyra. He owed her big-time for the happiness that she'd brought to his life. The least he could do was see if either of his parents were coming to the wedding.

With great trepidation, he dialed his mother's number. She immediately answered.

"Hello, Mother."

"Cristo, don't you ever answer your phone these days?"

She'd called him? This was news to him. He was certain there weren't any voice mails from her. He wouldn't forget something like that. "What's the matter? Is it Father?"

"Your father is fine."

"That's good." Why had he gone and jumped to conclusions? Maybe because his mother didn't call often and certainly not repeatedly. "What did you need?"

"It isn't what I need, but rather, what do you need? After all, you're the one getting married."

"I...I don't need anything." Well, that wasn't exactly true. He needed answers, but he wasn't sure his mother was the person to give them to him.

He needed to know if he was putting too much stock into building a lasting relationship with Kyra. When it was all over, would they end up cold and distant like his parents? The thought chilled him to the bone. He didn't think he could bear it if they did. And he certainly wouldn't want his children growing up in such an icy atmosphere.

He tried to think back to a time when his parents had been warm and affectionate with each other. Surely they must have been at one point. For the life of him, he couldn't recall his father sweeping his mother into his arms and planting a kiss on her lips just because he loved her and wanted to show her. How could they coexist all of these years with such distance between them?

"Mother, can I ask you a question?"

"You can ask, but I don't know if I'll have an answer for you."

His mother was a very reserved woman. She didn't sit down with a cup of coffee and spill her guts. Whatever she felt, she held it in. Maybe she was more like his father than Cristo bothered to notice before now.

"When you and Father married, were things different in the beginning?"

"Different? How so?"

"You know, was he always a workaholic?" Cristo just couldn't bring himself to say *icy* and *cold*.

"Your father made it perfectly clear from the start that his work would always come first."

"And you were all right with that?"

There was a slight pause. "I understood how important his work was to him."

"What about Max's accident? Did that change him?" What Cristo really wanted to know was if he was responsible in some way for his father's chilly distance from his own family.

This time there was a distinct pause. "The accident changed everyone. You included. But you can't blame yourself. It was an accident."

"That's not what Father thinks."

There was a poignant pause. "What your father thinks is that the accident was his fault. But he doesn't know what to do with all of that guilt and grief so he projects it on those closest to him. It creates a barrier around him, keeping us all out. He no longer thinks he deserves our love."

"Really?" Cristo had never gotten that impression. Had he been reading his father wrong all of this time?

"I think your father is afraid of losing someone else he loves, including you. I can't promise he'll ever be the father you want—the father you deserve—but sometimes you have to accept people flaws and all. Cristo, I'd love nothing more than our family to heal."

To heal there had to be forgiveness—a letting go of the past. Would his father be able to do that?

More important, would Cristo be able to do it? Could he let go of his guilt over Max's death?

Cristo surprised himself when he realized that Kyra had opened his eyes and shown him the importance of family. Kyra had also pointed out a fact that both he and his father had been overlooking—Max wouldn't have wanted this big rift in the family. He was forever the peacemaker.

Maybe the best way to honor Max's memory was to swallow his pride and make peace with his father. But there was something he needed to know first. "Mother, is that what Father wants, too? For the family to be together again?"

There was a poignant pause. "I think he does, even if he can't bring himself to say the words."

His mother was only guessing. Of course his father wouldn't admit that he needed his family. That would make him look weak. "I don't know how you do it."

"Do what?"

"Make excuses for him and give him the benefit of the doubt. Do you really love him that much?"

There was suddenly a distinct chilliness in her voice. "Cristo, what are all of these questions about? Are you having second thoughts about your wedding?"

He was definitely having doubts, but not as she was thinking. He had to make a choice—his work or his bride. He couldn't have them both in equal portions. One had to outweigh the other. But could he let go of his work—his meetings and his endless phone calls—in order to put Kyra first in his life?

"Cristo, you're worrying me. What are you thinking?"

"That I don't want to end up like my father." It wasn't until the words were out of his mouth that he realized he'd voiced his worst fear. And he didn't have any idea how his mother would take such a statement.

"You have a good heart. Follow it. It won't let you down."

His mother rarely handed out advice, so for her to say this, she had to really believe it. His mother thought he had a good heart. A spot in his chest warmed. Maybe what he needed now was to have more faith in his love for Kyra.

"Thank you. This talk helped. I know exactly what to do. I've got to go."

After getting off the phone, he knew the only way to prove his love for Kyra was real would be to turn his back on the deal with Stravos. His heart beat faster. But how could he do that when he had worked so hard to make this deal a reality? He clenched his hands. How could he give up his chance to finally prove himself to his father—to earn his father's respect?

But then Kyra's smile came to mind and his fisted hands relaxed. He remembered the way her eyes lit up when she was happy. He conjured up the memory of her melodious laughter and the way it relaxed him. She knew what was important in life—family and love.

He had to trust in his love for her.

The rest would work itself out.

CHAPTER EIGHTEEN

WASN'T THIS EVERY little girl's dream?

Kyra turned in a circle in front of the large mirrors that had been specially delivered to her suite. The slim-fitting snow-white lace-and-organza bridal gown was divine. This was her final fitting and she didn't think the dress needed another stitch. It was absolutely perfect. The neckline dipped, giving just a hint of her cleavage. The bodice hugged her waist. She smiled at her reflection, imagining what it'd be like to walk down the aisle and have Cristo waiting for her.

She'd tried on countless wedding dresses from frilly ball gowns to hip-hugging mermaid-style dresses. They were either too flouncy, too clingy or too revealing. She had started to think she'd never find the right dress.

It wasn't until her frustration had reached the breaking point that she stopped and wondered why she was working so hard to find the perfect dress for a fake wedding. Why was it so important to her?

As of yet, she didn't have an answer—at least none she was willing to accept.

The wedding was only two days away and Cristo had yet to call it off. She didn't understand why, especially now that her uncle had stated their marriage would have no bearing on his decision to sell the hotel chain. Or was Cristo hoping to really go through with the wedding? Did he think by marrying her that her uncle would feel obligated to follow through with the sale?

A frown pulled at her lips. Was she merely a means to an end? The thought made her stomach lurch. Or was she making too much of things—letting her imagination run amok?

She inhaled a deep, calming breath. That must be it, because Cristo had been nothing but charming and thoughtful. He wouldn't hurt her. It was bride's nerves—even if she wasn't truly a bride. And besides, with Cristo holding off on canceling the wedding there was still a chance his parents would make an appearance. Kyra had even sent them a note pleading with them to come for their son's sake. She never heard back.

A knock at the door curtailed her thoughts. The suite had been a hub of activity all morning in preparation for the big day. She'd never had so many people fuss over her. It was a bit intoxicating. If only it was real…

She spun around one more time, enjoying the breezy feel of the luxurious material. She wondered what Cristo would think of it. Would he want something more traditional? Or perhaps he'd rather she wear something more daring—more revealing? Kyra sighed. The truth was she didn't know what he'd think and she never would.

"Hello, Kyra."

Oh, no! It can't be.

Kyra spun around, finding her mother standing in the doorway of the suite. Her arms were crossed. That was never, ever a good sign.

"Mom, what are you doing here? I didn't know you were flying in."

"You would have known if you'd ever check your messages. But I guess we're even now because I didn't know my own daughter was getting married."

Kyra glanced down at her wedding dress. "I can explain."

Her mother's gaze narrowed. "I can't wait to hear this."

Kyra inwardly groaned. Could this day possibly get any worse?

"Explain what?" Cristo came to a stop next to her mother.

This time Kyra groaned aloud. It was her fault. She shouldn't have tempted fate. Now look at what she'd brought upon herself, her mother and her fake groom all in the same room. Wasn't this cozy?

Her mother turned to Cristo. "And you would be?"

"Cristo Kiriakas. The groom. And you would be?"

"The mother of the bride." Her painted red lips

pressed together in a firm line of disapproval. Her gaze flickered between Cristo and Kyra. "And now you've ruined everything."

A look of bewilderment filled Cristo's wide eyes. "Excuse me. I don't understand. What did I ruin?"

"Surely someone must have told you the groom can't see the bride in her wedding gown. Now go. Get. You can't be here."

Cristo's brows drew together and his voice deepened. "This is my suite and no one orders me around."

"Must you be so stubborn? Don't you know being here is bad luck? Come back later. My girl and I have some catching up to do."

He sent Kyra a questioning look. She shrugged. Right about now, her face felt as if it was on fire. This just couldn't be happening. This had to be some sort of nightmare and soon she'd wake up.

Cristo sent her a reassuring smile, letting her know he had everything in hand. "I think she looks absolutely beautiful in her gown." He glanced up at the ceiling. "See, no lightning strikes. I think we're safe."

"Really? Are you really going to stand there and mock me?" Her mother sent him an I-dare-you-to-argue-with-me glare.

Kyra inwardly groaned. She knew that look all too well. Cristo would lose and it wouldn't be pretty. Kyra rushed over to the counter and grabbed her phone. Reinforcements were needed and fast.

Mop&Glow007 (Kyra): 911...suite

MaidintheShade347 (Sofia): What's wrong?

Mop&Glow007 (Kyra): Everything. Hurry.

Tension filled the room.

"Mom, what are you doing here?" Kyra tried to redirect the conversation.

For a moment, her mother didn't move. Eventually, she turned to Kyra. "You surely didn't think I was going to let my only child walk down the aisle without me."

"But I'm not—" Cristo sent her an icy stare that froze the words in the back of her mouth.

Her mother's perfectly plucked brows drew together. "You're not what?"

"I'm not," she said as she glanced at Cristo, who shook his head, "getting married right now."

Her mother sighed. "And you expect me to believe that while you're standing here in your wedding dress? I know you're mad at me, but were you really going to get married without telling me?"

Kyra shrugged. She honestly didn't have an answer because she'd never thought about it, since this wedding was never going to take place. But with Cristo signaling for her to keep quiet about the fake engagement, she couldn't tell her mother the truth right now. And if her mother learned the truth, word would spread quickly. The scandal they desperately wanted to avoid would become a reality. So Kyra said nothing. *What a mess.*

"Mom, how did you know about the wedding?"

"I read it in the paper just like everyone else. Honestly, Kyra, do you know how it made me feel to learn about your engagement that way?"

Kyra sent Cristo a puzzled look. He'd promised that news of their engagement wouldn't be in the United States papers. He shrugged innocently.

"Kyra, what's really going on? Are you pregnant?"

"What? No! Mother!" The heat in her face amplified.

Her mother's suspicious stare moved from her to Cristo and back again. "I'm only saying what others will think with such a rushed wedding."

"That's it. I've heard enough." Cristo stepped up to her mother. "You can't come in here and upset Kyra. I think you've already caused her enough pain."

"Her pain? What about mine? She abandoned me and now she's trying to get married behind my back—"

"That's enough!" Cristo's voice held a steely edge. "Kyra has done nothing but love you and do everything she could to help you. It's you who owes her an apology."

Her mother gaped at him, but no words passed her lips.

"Kyra, I'm here. What's the emergency?" Sofia came to an abrupt halt in the open doorway. Her gaze moved rapidly between Cristo and Kyra's mother. "Oh. Hi, Mrs. Pappas."

For an awkward moment, no one spoke. The tension was thick in the room as Cristo and her mother continued to stare at each other as though in some power struggle.

Sofia sent Kyra a what-do-I-do-now look.

Kyra snapped out of her shocked stupor. "Sofia, why don't you give my mother a tour of the resort while I get out of this dress."

"I don't want a tour," her mother announced emphatically. "I want to know why you're standing there in your wedding gown in front of the groom. There's still time to fix this. We can find another dress—"

"Mom, no. This dress is perfect."

Her mother gave the dress due consideration and then nodded. "It was perfect, but now it's jinxed."

"It is not. I love it. Now, please go with Sofia." Before her mother could argue, Kyra added, "Really, Mom, go ahead. I have a few things to discuss with the seamstress and then I'll be free."

"But what about him?" Her mother nodded toward Cristo.

"He's not superstitious and neither am I. We'll make our own luck."

"Well, I never..." With a loud huff, her mother turned and stormed out of the room.

Sofia sent her one last distressed look.

Kyra mouthed, *Sorry.*

Once they were gone, Cristo shut the door. "Would you mind explaining what just happened here?"

"Tornado Margene blew into town, huffing and puffing." Kyra stepped down from the pedestal, anxious to get out of the dress.

"So I've seen. But what is she doing here?"

"Why are you asking me? You're the one who promised not to put our wedding announcement in the New York papers. If you want someone to blame for this fiasco, look in the mirror."

"I didn't do it." When she continued to look skeptical, he continued. "Why would I? It just complicates things further." He paused as though a thought had just come to him.

"What is it? Don't hold back now." She approached him.

"Considering the timing of your mother's visit, I'm going to guess my mother received her wedding invitation and arranged for the press to be informed. It would be something she'd do. She's always taking care of details like that. She doesn't know we're not—well, um…that the marriage—"

"Isn't real," Kyra whispered, finishing the sentence though it left an uneasy feeling in her stomach.

He raked his fingers through his hair. "This certainly complicates things."

"You think? And I've got my finals tonight." She should be studying this afternoon, not trying to appease her mother.

Cristo's face took on a concerned look. "Can you get an extension?"

She shook her head while catching the anxious look on the seamstress's face. "I've got to change clothes. I'll be back. Don't go anywhere. We aren't done talking."

This arrangement couldn't go on. She shouldn't have agreed to it in the first place. In the end, it hadn't worked out for Cristo after all. She felt awful for him.

Would Cristo understand when she called everything off? Would they still be on friendly terms? Or would they go their separate ways and never see each other again? The thought of never seeing Cristo again tore at her heart.

But she realized that's the way it needed to be. He had his work. She had her family. That had to be enough.

Kyra wasn't just beautiful.

She was stunning in her wedding dress. Like a princess.

Cristo paced the length of the living room. Over and over. Her mother making a surprise appearance certainly wasn't how he'd planned for their talk to start.

For days now he'd been trying to decide how to propose for real. At last he had everything sorted out. That was until her mother showed up. Why did her mother pick today of all days to fly in?

He stopped and stared down the hallway. There was no sign of Kyra. What was taking her so long? He paced some more.

He envisioned telling Kyra his decision to make this marriage authentic. Her face would light up with joy as she rushed into his arms and kissed him. Excitement swelled in his chest at the mere idea of it. He'd promise her that they could face anything as long as they were together and she'd agree. Life would be perfect. Okay, maybe that was stretching things with her mother being at the resort, but it would all work out. It had to.

At last Kyra emerged from her room in a pair of peach capris with a white lace tank top. Her hair was in a twist and piled atop her head with a clip. She looked absolutely adorable. Thankfully the seamstress had made a hasty departure.

Cristo drew in a deep steadying breath and then slowly blew it out. "Kyra, we need to talk—"

"If this is about my mother, I'm sorry for accusing you of letting the cat out of the bag."

"It's okay—"

"No, it isn't. I jumped to conclusions and I shouldn't have." Her gaze didn't meet his. "There's something I have to tell you. I know we made a deal, but I…I can't go through with this. I have to be honest with my mother—with everyone."

"I understand."

Her head jerked upward and her wide-eyed gaze met his. "You do? You understand?"

His gaze moved to the windows. Suddenly he felt the walls closing in on him. Or maybe it was a case of anxiety. He'd never considered it before now, but what if Kyra turned him down? What would he do then?

"Cristo? Did you hear me?"

"I have an idea. How about some sunshine and fresh air?"

Her brows arched. "What about our talk?"

"We'll talk. I promise." He moved toward the door. "Come on."

"Cristo, I can't. If you hadn't noticed, my mother is here."

"She can wait. This can't."

He led her to the elevator, out the back entrance and down a windy path to the beach area. Maybe he should have rehearsed what he was going to say to her. Where did he even begin? His jaw tensed. What if he made a mess of things?

Kyra touched his arm. "Hey, what's wrong?"

He glanced over at her. Concern reflected in her eyes. The words wouldn't come. They caught in the back of his throat.

"Just relax." She slipped her hand in his. "Whatever it is, we'll deal with it."

His frantic thoughts centered. All he could think about was how her smooth fingertips moved slowly over his palm, sending a heady sensation shooting up to his chest and farther. His anxious, rushed thoughts smoothed out. He could do this. Anything was possible with Kyra by his side. They were a team.

Hand in hand they walked along the path away from the crowded beachfront. This time around, he didn't want an audience for what he was about to say. He just needed Kyra.

Alone at last, he turned to her. "I have something I need to tell you."

Worry lines creased her beautiful face. "It's okay. I know what you want to talk about."

"You do?" Was he that obvious? He didn't think so but, then again, Kyra knew him better than anyone. He'd opened up to her far more than he'd ever done with anyone.

"It's my mother. Don't worry. I'll send her packing—"

"No, it's not her. And you don't have to ask her to leave on my account. In fact, it might be better if she stayed—"

"Why? Are your parents coming for the wedding, too?"

He shook his head. "My mother called. Neither she nor my father will be attending. She blamed it on my father's hectic work schedule."

"I take it you don't believe her?"

He shrugged. "It doesn't matter. I don't need them here. But it might be nice if your mother stayed—"

"Stayed? Why do you keep saying that?"

He took both of Kyra's hands in his. "It's okay. You don't have to worry. I have a plan."

"A plan? Isn't that what just blew up in our faces? First with my uncle and now with my mother—"

"I guess you wouldn't exactly call it a plan."

Frustration reflected in Kyra's eyes. "Would you please explain what you're talking about?"

He was beating around the subject and making this conversation far more complicated than it needed to be. "The truth is, I called Nikolaos today. And I withdrew my offer to buy the hotels."

"What? But why? That deal means everything to you."

"Because somewhere along the way, you taught me there are other things more important than business and beating my father at his own game."

"I did that?"

Cristo nodded. "You taught me that and a lot more."

He dropped down on one knee. "I know I am supposed to have a ring when I do this, but seeing as you're already wearing it—"

"Cristo, get up!" Her eyes widened with surprise. "What are you doing?"

"You know what I'm doing. I'm proposing, if you'll let me get the words out."

"You can't. This isn't right." She pulled her hands from his.

Wait. What? She was supposed to be jumping into his arms. Lathering his face with kisses. Not standing there looking as though she was about to burst into tears at any second.

He was so confused. He thought at last he'd gotten things right—choosing love over business. But it still wasn't working out with a happily-ever-after.

Where had he gone wrong?

CHAPTER NINETEEN

THIS COULDN'T BE HAPPENING.

Cristo was saying all of the right things at exactly the wrong time.

Kyra took a step back. She couldn't—she wouldn't—be the woman he sacrificed everything for. The fact he'd withdrawn his offer for the Stravos hotels was too much. Though she loved him dearly, she couldn't let him turn his life upside down to be with her. She wouldn't be able to bear it when later he ended up resenting her.

"I can't do this." Her hands trembled as she slipped the diamond ring from her finger and pressed it into his palm.

"Kyra—"

"I'm so sorry." She turned on shaky legs, hoping they'd carry her back to the hotel.

"Don't walk away. Kyra, I know you care. Why are you doing this to us?"

She paused. If she was honest with him, he would just explain away her worries. He'd be more concerned about the here and now. He wouldn't give the future due consideration. But she could. She had to be the strong one—for his sake.

With every bit of willpower, she turned back and met the pained look on his face. "You have to understand that we've let ourselves get caught up in this fairy tale. Neither of us has been thinking straight."

"That's not true." His eyes pleaded with her.

"Everyone can see we don't belong together. Your parents can't even be bothered to meet me. Why can't you see that this is a mistake?"

"My parents know nothing of love. If they ever loved each other, it was over years ago. But I do love you. I guess the real question is, do you love me?"

Kyra's gaze lowered to the ground. "You need and deserve more than I can give you. You're an amazing guy. Someday you'll find the right lady and she'll make you happy. You'll see—"

"What I see is you refusing to admit that you love me, too." He reached out to her.

Kyra sidestepped his touch. She knew that if he touched her—held her close—she'd lose her strength. She'd never be able to let him go—to let him find happiness. "I don't want to hurt you. I never wanted to do that. But you have to realize that this dream world we created isn't real. You and I as a couple, it isn't real."

His eyes grew dark and a wall came down in them, blocking her out. Even though they were standing beneath the warm Greek sun, a shiver ran across her skin.

"And that's it? You're done with us?" His voice vibrated with frustration.

"I think it's best we call the wedding off immediately and go our separate ways before we hurt each other any more."

He stared at her long and hard, but she couldn't tell what he was thinking. And then he cursed under his breath and started back toward the hotel—alone.

Kyra pressed a hand to her mouth, stifling a sob. She couldn't let her emotions bubble over now. She had to keep it together a little longer—until Cristo was out of sight.

He would never know how hard it was to turn him away. But she couldn't make the divide between him and his parents even wider—because they'd made it clear with their silence that they didn't approve of her. She was a nobody by their social standards. Her chest ached at the thought they wouldn't even give her a chance.

And now Cristo had sacrificed his chance to merge the Glamour Hotel chain and the Stravos Star Hotels. The enormity of the gesture finally struck her and a tear dropped onto her cheek. No one had ever sacrificed something so important for her. How was she ever going to move on without him?

Kyra dashed away the tears. Somehow she had to make things right once again for Cristo.

But how?

Her phone chimed. She pulled it from her pocket.

MaidintheShade347 (Sofia): Do you want to hang out?

Mop&Glow007 (Kyra): Can't.

MaidintheShade347 (Sofia): Busy with Cristo?

Mop&Glow007 (Kyra): No.

MaidintheShade347 (Sofia): No? What's up?

Mop&Glow007 (Kyra): It's over.

MaidintheShade347 (Sofia): What's over?

Mop&Glow007 (Kyra): Everything.

MaidintheShade347 (Sofia): Where are you?

Mop&Glow007 (Kyra): The beach.

MaidintheShade347 (Sofia): I'll be right there.

Kyra moved to the sand and sank down on it. It didn't matter if Sofia showed up or not. No one could fix this. No one at all. She'd done what was needed. Somehow she had to learn to live with the consequences, as painful as they were.

CHAPTER TWENTY

THE WEDDING WAS TOMORROW.

Correction. The wedding was supposed to be tomorrow.

Still in yesterday's clothes, Cristo paced back and forth in the empty suite. Kyra hadn't returned to their suite since they'd spoken yesterday—when he'd made a complete and utter fool of himself. He'd never begged a woman not to leave him. And yet, baring his soul to her hadn't seemed to faze her. He didn't understand her. He didn't understand any of this.

Kyra was different from any other woman he'd ever known. And he was different when he was with her. She brought out the best in him. And now that she was gone, he had all of the time in the world to catch up with business, but he didn't have the heart to do it. For the first time ever, he'd lost his zealousness for making boardroom deals.

What was wrong with him?

So what if a woman had dumped him? He knew better than to invest too heavily in a relationship.

He knew they were likely to turn sour at a moment's notice just like his parents' unhappy union.

He should be happy he'd gotten out of the engagement unscathed. He could have ended up married to a woman who didn't love him. That would definitely be a road map to unhappiness.

How could he have let himself think any of it was real?

They'd been having fun. They'd been laughing and talking. That was all. He'd let himself get caught in those smiles of hers that lit up her whole face. He'd fooled not only those around them, but himself. He'd let himself believe in a fantasy of them creating a lasting relationship. And absolutely none of it had been real.

No matter how hard he tried, he couldn't make himself believe that last part. It had been real, at least for him. And that was what made this so difficult.

Thank goodness his father didn't know what a mess he'd made of things. It would have just reinforced his father's opinion that he was incapable of making important decisions—decisions for a multimillion-dollar business.

Cristo's hands balled as every muscle in his body stiffened. He was losing his edge. And that couldn't happen. He had to get a grip on his life and get it back on track. But how? It was as if by losing Kyra, he'd lost his rudder.

A knock at the door jarred him from his thoughts.

Kyra!

His heart raced. His palms grew clammy. He had to handle this the right way. He would be calm, cool and collected. He inhaled a deep breath and then blew it out.

His footsteps were swift and direct. He yanked the door open. "You came back."

Niko's brow knit together. "I wasn't here before."

"Oh. Never mind. I thought you were someone else." Cristo inwardly groaned as he turned and walked farther into the room.

Niko closed the door behind him. "So, are you ready for tonight?"

"Ready for what?"

"How could you forget? Tonight's your bachelor party. Your last night of freedom."

In truth, Cristo had forgotten, but he wasn't about to admit it. He wasn't about to let Niko read too much into his forgetfulness. "Sorry. I've been busy."

Niko glanced around the suite. "You don't look busy now. Want to grab some dinner before the party?"

Cristo rubbed his stiff neck. "I'm not hungry."

Niko sat down. "So tell me what's wrong."

"Why do you think something's wrong?"

"I didn't want to say anything, but you look like hell. So do you want to tell me what is going on?"

Cristo spun around and faced his friend, who had agreed to be his best man. Cristo hadn't asked him to fulfill the role because of the potential business deal, but rather because they'd struck up an easy friendship. Plus, Niko was going to be family and what better way to draw Kyra into her newfound family than to invite her cousin to be part of the wedding?

But so much had changed since that decision had been made. Cristo might as well let Niko know it was over. What was the point in holding back? Soon everyone would know the truth.

Cristo balled up his hands. "The…the wedding… it's off."

"What? But why? You and Kyra looked so happy together at dinner the other week."

Cristo choked down his bruised ego and pushed past his scarred heart to tell Niko the whole horrible story. He started with Kyra's mother making a surprise appearance and how her mother had lied to her. Then he mentioned the disastrous proposal. Cristo had hoped that by getting it off his chest he'd start to feel better about everything. But in the end, he didn't feel any better. In fact, he felt worse—much worse.

Niko looked him directly in the eyes. "Do you love her?"

Cristo sank down on the couch. "I thought I did but…but I was wrong."

"You don't believe that any more than I do. I know your ego is wounded. Any man's would be. But is it worth walking away from the love of your life?"

"You're just saying that because she's your cousin."

"No, I'm not. I'm saying this because I've never seen a man look so miserable. Look at you. You're an absolute mess."

Cristo glanced down at his wrinkled clothes. He ran a hand over his hair, finding it scattered. And he didn't even have to check his jaw to know he had heavy stubble. His face was already getting itchy.

"Have you eaten anything recently?"

"I'm not hungry." Though his empty stomach growled its disagreement, he just didn't have any interest in food.

"There has to be a way to fix this." Niko sighed as he leaned back. "Did you ever consider she might have had a case of bridal nerves?"

Cristo shook his head. "It's not that."

"What do you think went wrong?"

"I don't know. That's what I spent all night and today trying to figure out. In the beginning, I never intended to care about her, but somewhere along the way this pretend relationship became the genuine thing."

"Did you tell Kyra this?"

"I started to, but she cut me off and told me I was making a mistake. She thinks everything I'm feeling is just an illusion."

"And is it?"

He shook his head. "It's real. I even called your grandfather and withdrew my offer to buy the hotel chain, hoping to prove my sincerity to her. But it didn't seem to faze her. In fact, it had the opposite effect."

"Trust me. I'm no expert on women and love, but if she means that much to you, you should go after her. Make her understand this isn't some illusion—that your feelings for her are real."

Cristo rubbed his neck again. "I don't know. Why would she believe me this time?"

"Maybe because this time you aren't going to blindside her with a proposal right after an emotional run-in with her mother. Maybe by now she realizes she made a monumental mistake, but she's too embarrassed to come back and face you."

Niko's words struck a chord in him, but Cristo's ego still stood in the way. One rejection was bad enough. Being rejected twice was just too much. "Why should I go after her when she was the one to back out of the wedding in the first place?"

Niko arched a brow. "Would you give up this easily on a business deal?"

Cristo inwardly groaned. His friend knew how driven he was, but that was business and this was… was different.

When Cristo didn't answer, Niko continued. "Wouldn't you try to do everything in your power to secure the deal—even if it meant risking a second rejection?"

Cristo knew all along that Niko was right. At this point, he didn't have anything more to lose. But he did have a chance to gain everything that was truly important. It was a chance to hold Kyra in his arms once more. A chance to gaze into her eyes and tell her how much he loved her. His love for her trumped his wounded pride.

Cristo jumped to his feet. "Don't call off the bachelor party." He started for the door. "I'll catch up with you later."

"Cristo, wait." When he turned around, Niko added, "Don't you think you should shower first?"

"I don't have time for that now. I have something far more important to do."

Now that he had a plan, he couldn't wait around. He had to go to Kyra. He had to apologize for throwing everything at her at once.

At last he realized he'd been so caught up in his own feelings and plans that Kyra's feelings hadn't registered. It hadn't struck him until now how her mother's appearance would make Kyra feel vulnerable. Instead of being there for her, he'd been pushing his own agenda as if their marriage was some sort of business deal.

Now he needed to apologize and be there to support Kyra as she dealt with her mother.

Whatever she needed, he'd do it.

He loved her.

He would wait for her…as long as she needed.

CHAPTER TWENTY-ONE

"STOP! I DON'T need to hear this. It's over. Done."

Kyra glared at Sofia, willing her to drop the subject of her now-defunct wedding. She couldn't take any more of being badgered by her best friend and her mother. They were getting on her case for calling off the wedding. They just didn't understand. She'd lost the only man she'd ever loved and to compound matters she'd just completed her finals even though she'd hardly been able to concentrate on them. Thankfully her test results wouldn't be in for another week.

She sat on Sofia's couch and stabbed a spoon in the now-soft ice cream. She could only deal with one tragedy at a time. And missing Cristo was as much as she could take at the moment.

"Obviously you need to listen to somebody as you're not making any sense." Her mother crossed her arms and frowned at her.

"And you're lucky I'm even speaking to you after the way you lied and manipulated me. How could you do it?"

The color drained from her mother's face. "I told you I'm sorry."

Kyra swirled the spoon in the ice cream. "And that's supposed to fix everything?"

"No." Her mother sounded defeated. "I was wrong. After your father died, I wasn't thinking clearly. I couldn't bear to be alone."

"Why couldn't you have just said that instead of creating elaborate lies and scheming to get me to move back in with you?"

Her mother lowered her arms and then laced her fingers together. When she spoke, her voice was soft. "You had your own life. Your own friends. I thought you'd say no. And I would be all alone for the first time in my life." Tears splashed onto her mother's cheeks. "I was so lost without your father. He was my best friend."

The anger Kyra had been nursing the past few weeks melted away. As her mother softly cried, Kyra set aside her ice cream in order to put her arms around her. No matter what, she still loved her. "It's okay, Mom. You aren't going to lose me. Ever."

Her mother straightened and Sofia, looking a bit awkward, handed her some tissues. Her mother's watery gaze moved from Sofia back to Kyra. "Really? You forgive me?"

"I'm working on it." It was the best she could offer for now. Her mother's lies had cut deeply. It would take time for the wounds to completely heal.

"But you have to promise to always be honest with me…even if you're scared."

Her mother nodded as the tears welled up again. "I promise." She dabbed the tissues to her damp cheeks and then turned her bloodshot eyes to Kyra. "But you can't let what I've done ruin your future with Cristo. I've seen the way he looks at you. He loves you—"

"Mom, don't! That isn't going to help. What's done is done. I don't want to talk about it."

Her mother got to her feet. "You're making a mistake."

Once her mother retreated to the tiny balcony of Sofia's efficiency apartment, Kyra flounced back against the couch. No one understood she'd done what was necessary. Cristo was better off without her.

Sofia moved to stand in front of her. She planted her hands on her hips. "You aren't going to scare me off. So don't try."

Kyra retrieved the carton of rocky road from the end table and took another bite. "Why doesn't anyone believe this is for the best?"

"Because you don't believe it yourself or you wouldn't be shoveling that ice cream in your mouth with a serving spoon."

"That's not true. It's a soup spoon." She glanced down, realizing she'd single-handedly wiped out half of the large container. This wasn't good. She set aside the melting ice cream and stood. "I need some air."

"Want some company?"

She shook her head. "I have some thinking to do."

"Think about the fact you might have been wrong about Cristo. He really loves you."

"You're just saying that because you want to believe in happily-ever-after." Kyra headed for the door.

"I never stopped believing in them. It's just that they are for other people, like you, not me. I have a habit of picking out the wrong guys."

Kyra opened the door and stepped into the quiet hallway before turning back. "You'll surprise yourself one of these days and find yourself a keeper."

"Oh, yeah, listen to who's talking. You've got yourself a keeper and you're tossing him back."

As Kyra walked away, she realized Sofia was right. Cristo was a keeper for someone—just not her.

The sun was setting as she walked along the path that snaked its way along the beach. The lingering golden rays bounced off the water, making it sparkle like an array of glittering diamonds—like the one that used to be on her finger. She glanced down at her bare hand. Tears stung the backs of her eyes. She blinked them away. Her emotions felt as though they'd been shoved through a cheese grater. Why did doing the right thing have to be so difficult?

As she walked, she kept replaying snippets of her

time with Cristo. She loved how he'd started to let down his guard with her—how he'd started to enjoy life instead of going from one meeting to the next. She hoped now he wouldn't revert to his old ways. There was so much more to life than business—even if his future wasn't with her.

"Kyra."

She knew the sound of his voice as well as she knew her own. It was Cristo. How had he found her? Silly question. Sofia and her mother would have tripped over themselves to tell him where to find her.

She turned to him, too exhausted and miserable to put on a smile. But when her gaze landed on him, she found she wasn't the only one who wasn't doing well. Cristo's hair was a mess. His suit looked as though it had been in a hamper for a week. Wait. Weren't those the same clothes from yesterday? And then there were the dark shadows beneath his bloodshot eyes.

She stepped up to him. "Cristo, what's the matter?"

He didn't say anything. He just stared at her. All the while, her concern mounted. Maybe he was ill. Maybe something had happened to his family.

"Cristo, please say something. You're scaring me. Is everything all right?"

"No. Everything is not all right."

"Tell me what it is. I'll do what I can to help."

"Do you truly mean that?"

"Of course." She had already sacrificed her heart and her happiness for him, what was a little more?

CHAPTER TWENTY-TWO

CRISTO WANTED TO believe her.

He wanted to believe Kyra had at last come to her senses.

He wanted to believe she'd been caught off guard yesterday when he'd proposed. But the only way to find out was to put his scarred heart back on the line. His pulse raced and his palms grew moist.

With the lingering rays of the setting sun highlighting her beautiful face, he also noticed the sadness reflected in her eyes. Maybe Niko was right. Maybe too many surprises had been thrown at her yesterday. Maybe it had been bridal nerves. He sure hoped that's all it was.

Cristo stared deep into her eyes, knowing this would be the most important pitch of his life. "Kyra, I'm sorry about yesterday. I shouldn't have sprung that proposal on you after you had the shock of seeing your mother again. I was anxious." His head lowered. "I wasn't thinking clearly."

"It's okay. I'm not mad at you."

He lifted his head to see if she was telling him

the truth. In her eyes, he found utter sincerity. "So if you aren't upset, why did you push me away?"

"We don't belong together. These past weeks have been an amazing fantasy and you've been wonderful, but it can't last forever. Things end."

"Are you thinking about your mother and father?"

She shrugged but her gaze didn't quite meet his.

"Well, I'm not your father. And no, I can't promise you that we'll have fifty years together. But you can't predict we won't. The future is a big question mark. But there is one thing that I do know."

"What?"

"That I love you." When she went to protest, he pressed a finger to her lips. "And it isn't part of my imagination. It's a fact. I love the way you laugh. I love the way you can see the important things in life. And I love that you are forever putting other people's happiness ahead of your own."

She removed his finger from her mouth but not before pressing a kiss to it. "It's more than that. I know how much you want your father's approval. They will never approve of a nobody like me."

"First of all, you're not a nobody."

"You mean because I'm Nikolaos Stravos's long-lost great-niece?"

"No. Because you're a ray of sunshine who makes this world a better place just by being in it."

"But your parents—"

"Will come around."

"Really? They won't even come to our wedding.

I…I wrote them a note pleading with them to come to the wedding for you. And still they say nothing. I really thought I could get through to them."

His hands cupped her face. "See, there's another thing you've taught me—to quit working so hard to gain other people's approval. Fulfillment has to come from within—knowing that whatever I choose to do in life, I do it to the best of my ability."

"But they're your family."

"No. You're my family. I love you, Kyra. And I will be here to love you and support you."

There was a moment of silence. Oh, no. He prayed he'd gotten through to her.

"I do. I love you." Her eyes filled with unshed tears.

"I love you, too. And when you're ready, I have a question for you. But I won't pressure you. I'll wait. I'll wait for as long as it takes."

She sniffled and smiled up at him through her happy tears. "I'm ready now."

"You're sure?"

She nodded.

He slipped the ring from his pocket and held it out to her. "Kyra, will you marry me?"

She nodded as a tear splashed onto her cheek. "Yes. Yes, I will."

He'd never been so happy in his life. For so long, he thought seeking out bigger and better business deals would bring him the peace and happiness that he'd desired. How had he been so wrong?

"From this point forward, you and I are family." He leaned forward and pressed his lips to hers.

EPILOGUE

Next day...

"Talk about a perfect day."

"Do you really mean it?" Kyra looked up into her husband's handsome face as they swayed to a romantic ballad. All around them were wedding guests, smiling and talking.

"Of course I mean it. How could you doubt it?"

"It's just that I know this isn't how you'd been hoping things would turn out—"

He placed a finger to her lips, silencing her words. "We agreed we weren't going to discuss business today."

"I know. I just feel really bad you weren't able to work out the deal for the hotel chain. I think me turning out to be Nikolaos's great-niece hurt you instead of helped you."

Cristo arched a brow at her. "I've learned there are more important things in life than a successful business deal…such as an amazing wife and a monthlong honeymoon to look forward to."

Her heart swelled with love as she gazed into Cristo's mesmerizing eyes, and it was there she saw her future. "Do you know how much I love you?"

"Not as much as I love you." He leaned forward and pressed his lips to hers.

Being held in his strong arms and feeling his lips move over hers was something she'd never tire of. It was like coming home. Because no matter where they were, Cristo was her home, now and forever.

He led her from the dance floor and was about to get her a refreshment when Uncle Nikolaos approached them. She immediately noticed his face was markedly pale. "Uncle, are you feeling all right?"

He waved off her concern. "I'm fine. Just a little tired. I guess I'm not used to getting out and about. But enough about me. I wanted to congratulate you again. Your grandmother would have been so proud of you. You're such a beautiful bride."

"Thank you." Kyra leaned forward and pressed a kiss to his weathered cheek.

Uncle Nikolaos turned to Cristo and stuck out his hand. "Welcome to the family."

"Thank you, sir. Don't worry. I plan to make your niece very happy."

"I'm going to hold you to that promise. And I hope what I have to say won't distract you from the happiness you've found with Kyra, because nothing is more important than family."

Cristo wrapped his arm around her and pulled her close. "Trust me, sir. I've learned that lesson."

"Good. Then if you are still interested, expect a call soon to make the arrangements to have the Stravos Star Hotels sold to you. Consider it a wedding present."

For a moment no one spoke. At last Cristo found his voice. "Thank you. I am quite honored you trust me with the chain. I won't let you down."

"Thank your wife and Niko. They're both quite persuasive. An old man can only hold out so long."

All eyes turned to Niko, who had quietly stepped up and kissed Kyra's cheek. "Congratulations, cousin. You didn't do so bad in your choice of a groom."

"Thanks. I'm kind of fond of him." She flashed a big smile at Cristo.

Niko shook Cristo's hand. "Looks like we'll have a lot of details to sort through when you get back from your honeymoon."

"I'm hoping we won't have to wait that long—"

"Cristo, you promised." Kyra wasn't about to let him off the hook. This month away was supposed to be all about them, not his work.

He sent her a sheepish look. "I haven't forgotten. You won't even know that I'm working."

She really wanted to put her foot down, but she knew better than most how important this sale was to Cristo—it was his chance to step out from his father's shadow. She couldn't deny him this opportunity. "As long as you keep it to an hour in the morning while I'm enjoying my first cup of coffee and getting ready to tackle the day."

He held out his hand to her and they shook on it. "It's a deal."

She pulled on his hand until his face drew near hers and then she pressed her lips to his for a quick kiss. "Now it's a deal."

Everyone laughed.

"It was a beautiful ceremony," said a female voice.

Heads turned to find the new addition to their gathering.

He'd know that aristocratic voice anywhere.

"Mother." Cristo's voice rose with surprise mingled with happiness. "When did you get here?"

"We arrived a little bit ago."

We? Cristo glanced around. His gaze came to rest on his father. Was it his imagination or had his father aged considerably? There was considerable graying at the temples and the lines on the man's face were deeply etched.

When their gazes connected, Cristo detected the weariness reflected in his father's eyes. Cristo was so stunned by his father's appearance that he was at a loss for words. What did this all mean?

"Congratulations, son." His father held out his hand to him.

His father had taken time out of his busy schedule to be here. He wouldn't have done that voluntarily. Cristo suspected his mother had a lot to do with clearing his calendar. Cristo's gaze swung over to his mother, who had a hopeful gleam in her eyes. And then he noticed Kyra prodding him with her eyes to accept his father's gesture of goodwill.

He slipped his hand in his father's warm, firm grip. A smile eased the lines in his father's face. His father pulled him close and hugged him, clapping him on the back.

The hug didn't last long. Cristo quickly extracted himself from the awkward position. He hadn't been hugged by his father since he was a kid. He glanced at the ground unsure of what to do next.

"Thank you both for coming." Kyra stepped forward and held her hand out to his father, who in turn surprised everyone when he hugged her, too.

Cristo's mother stepped up next and gave Kyra a brief hug. "Welcome to the family."

Kyra stepped back to Cristo's side and took his hand in hers. "Thank you. I'm looking forward to getting to know you both."

"I was hoping you'd say that." His mother beamed. "When you return to the States, you're both invited to stay with us. You and I can house-hunt while the men are off tending to business."

Kyra smiled. "You have a date."

This was a surreal moment. Cristo tried to make sense of what had taken place just now. Sure, he was all hyped up by the rush of emotions from the wedding, but deep down, he had the feeling it was a new beginning for all of them.

His mother bestowed a warm smile on them. "May you both have a lifetime of happiness."

Cristo hoped the same thing. He wanted nothing more than to be able to make Kyra smile every day for the rest of their lives.

Kyra turned to her husband. Her husband. She loved the sound of those words. And she loved Cristo even more.

Tiny crystal bells placed at each table setting started to chime in unison, signaling it was time for the bride and groom to kiss. Kyra smiled as she turned to Cristo. He didn't waste any time sweeping her into his arms and planting a loving kiss upon her obliging lips. Her heart fluttered in her chest as if it was their first kiss.

Far too soon, he pulled away. Just then a romantic ballad started to play. Cristo held his arm out to her. "May I have this dance?"

As they moved around the dance floor, Kyra spotted Sofia at the bridal party table alone. Kyra frowned. She'd told her to bring a date, but Sofia had insisted there was no one she was interested in enough to ask to the wedding.

"What's the matter?" Cristo's voice drew Kyra out of her thoughts.

"Nothing."

"Come on now, I know you well enough to recognize the signs of you worrying about something or someone."

He was quite astute. "It's Sofia. She's all alone tonight and I feel bad. Perhaps I should have had you set her up with one of your friends."

"I'm glad you didn't ask."

Kyra stopped dancing and pulled back just far enough to look into her husband's eyes. "What's that supposed to mean? You don't think Sofia is good enough for your friends—"

"Slow down. That isn't what I meant at all."

"Then what did you mean?"

"That I'm not comfortable playing matchmaker. I think it's better when people find each other on their own. Like we did."

She hated to admit it, but he did have a good point. She moved back into his arms and started swaying to the music. "I suppose you're right."

"What did you say? I didn't quite hear you."

"I said you're right." And then she caught his sly smile. "Oh, you. You just wanted me to say you're right again."

"Hey, look." Cristo gazed off into the distance.

"Don't try to change the subject. You're just trying to get out of trouble."

"Is it working?"

"No." She sent him a teasing smile.

"But I'm serious. You should check out the bridal table again. I don't think you have to worry about Sofia having a boring time. Your cousin seems to have taken an interest in her."

"Really?" Kyra spun around to check it out. Sofia

was smiling. And so was Niko. "Do you really think anything will come of it?"

Cristo shrugged. "Hard to tell. Niko seems quite wary of relationships. But aren't you rushing things? They just met."

"True." She sighed. "I guess I just have romance on my mind."

"And so you should, Mrs. Kiriakas. This is just the beginning of our story."

"I can't wait to see what's next."

"Neither can I. I love you."

"I love you, too."

* * * * *

COMING NEXT MONTH FROM

HARLEQUIN® Romance

Available April 5, 2016

#4515 THE BILLIONAIRE'S BABY SWAP

The Montanari Marriages

by Rebecca Winters

Single mom Valentina Montanari and gorgeous billionaire Giovanni Laurito are stunned when they discover their tiny sons were swapped at birth! When they meet to reclaim their heirs, sparks fly. They've already fallen for each other's babies... Could this unexpected beginning create the perfect family?

#4516 THE WEDDING PLANNER'S BIG DAY

by Cara Colter

Tycoon Drew Jordan craves freedom, not commitment—he'll help arrange his brother's tropical wedding, but he'll never walk down the aisle himself. Yet when his clashes with wedding planner Becky English turn to moonlit kisses, can Becky help Drew see that happy endings do exist?

#4517 HOLIDAY WITH THE BEST MAN

Billionaires of London

by Kate Hardy

When billionaire best man Roland Devereux dances with Grace Faraday, he sweeps the bridesmaid off her feet. A temporary affair is all widower Roland can offer Grace, but on their whirlwind holiday their friendship becomes so much more...

#4518 TEMPTED BY HER TYCOON BOSS

by Jennie Adams

Sydney's masked ball is approaching, but hostess Cecilia Tomson is struggling to concentrate. Her gorgeous boss Linc MacKay, who rejected her years ago, has picked the *worst* moment to visit... Until one breathtaking kiss makes Cecilia wonder if Linc could be the man of her dreams!

YOU CAN FIND MORE INFORMATION ON UPCOMING HARLEQUIN® TITLES, FREE EXCERPTS AND MORE AT WWW.HARLEQUIN.COM.

HRLPCNM0316

SPECIAL EXCERPT FROM

Here is a sneak peek of
THE BILLIONAIRE'S BABY SWAP
by Rebecca Winters...

As long as they were both in the room with the babies, there were no tears. Only the sounds of the boys drinking rather noisily disturbed the peace and quiet. After burping him, Vito fell asleep first. She left him on her shoulder. He was her little angel. At this point she loved both babies so much she could hardly stand it.

Baby Ric finally passed out asleep with his bottle. Giovanni put him in his crib, then signaled Valentina to follow him into the bedroom. He patted the bed. She lay down on one side and put Vito in the middle. Giovanni stretched out on the other side. They turned toward the sleeping baby and smiled.

This was like playing house, except this wasn't a dollhouse and none of them were dolls.

Giovanni was a full grown, breathtaking male. Her bones melted with the way his eyes devoured her.

"Do you know this is the first time I've felt this content in years? How about you?"

She nodded. "Once I started undergraduate school, I put pressure on myself to succeed. The stress increased when I got into graduate school. Then I lost my mother, and her death devastated the whole family for a long time."

"I can only imagine," he commiserated.

"I could go to her about anything, Giovanni. She knew I suffered from an inferiority complex and told me I had to believe in myself no matter what." Her eyes smarted. "I'm wondering now, if she hadn't died, would I have gotten involved with Matteo?"

Giovanni reached across to give her arm a squeeze. "But if you hadn't, we wouldn't be lying here with our little boy who has brought so much joy into our lives. It's why I can't be sorry about my marriage to Tatania even though it ended. Ric is a living miracle."

"They both are," Valentina whispered.

"Thank you for accepting my invitation."

"I'm thrilled to be here. But it's getting late so, I'll say good-night and take Vito with me." She was loving this way too much. Using every bit of willpower, she rolled off the bed before gathering Vito in her arms.

Giovanni followed her out of his room to her bedroom down the hall. She felt his eyes on her as she put Vito into the crib. "Please remember this house is yours while you're here."

"I will. If you need help, I'll hear the crying and come."

"That works both ways, Valentina. *Buonanotte*."

After this wonderful evening she didn't want to say good-night, but to have stayed on his bed any longer would increase her desire to stay with him all night. She wanted to lie in his arms and be kissed senseless by him. How crazy was that!

"Good night."